LOST & FOUND

Rabbi Marc Gellman
and
Monsignor Thomas Hartman

Illustrated by Debbie Tilley

Lost & Found

—— A KID'S BOOK ——
FOR LIVING THROUGH LOSS

Morrow Junior Books · New York

Published by Morrow Junior Books
a division of William Morrow and Company, Inc.
1350 Avenue of the Americas, New York, NY 10019
www.williammorrow.com

Printed in the United States of America.

10 9 8 7 6 5 4 3 2 1

Library of Congress Cataloging-in-Publication Data
Gellman, Marc.
Lost and found: a kid's book for living through loss / Marc Gellman
and Thomas Hartman; illustrated by Debbie Tilley.
p. cm.
Summary: Describes different kinds of losses—losing possessions,
competitions, health, trust, and the permanent loss because of death—
and discusses how to handle these situations.
ISBN 0-688-15752-1
1. Loss (Psychology)—Religious aspects—Christianity—Juvenile
literature.   2. Death—Religious aspects—Christianity—Juvenile
literature.   [1. Loss (Psychology).   2. Death.]   I. Hartman, Thomas.
II. Tilley, Debbie ill.   III. Title.   BV4905.2.G44 1999
248.8'6'0834—dc21   98-27779   CIP AC

For Cal Kleinman in this world,
and for Joseph Cardinal Bernardin in the world to come,
both of whom have kept us on the path of finding

A Word to Adults about This Book

This is a book about many things a young person may lose in his or her life. Each chapter deals with a specific loss, beginning with the loss of little things like a game or a toy and moving through to the loss of life. We wrote each chapter to be shared with children approximately eight through twelve in age, or to be read alone by the children. Our deep hope is that the book might become a way to begin or continue family discussions about loss and about the way we must all learn to move through it to some greater wisdom about life.

The idea that loss is an opportunity to gain new wisdom is, we believe, both healing and true. Our lives are shaped perhaps more by the ways we handle life's hardships than by the ways we handle life's triumphs. It's often hard to see loss as an opportunity for wisdom, but it is essential. Otherwise, we are left with just the pain of loss and not the lessons we must learn in order to grow.

In this book we deal with many kinds of loss. Death is of course the most painful loss. By presenting death as a kind of extra big and extra painful loss, we hope to support and encourage the healing of children through their grief. Even children who have never faced death can understand that they have faced and overcome other losses in their lives, and this can help build confidence, courage, and hope in facing the biggest loss life can present. There is a tendency in us all, and children especially, to see our losses as ultimate and irrevocable. Our book tries to send the gentle message that our hardships, no matter how deeply felt, are not the end of us.

We also stress in this book that loss presents a chance to learn compassion. To feel another person's pain is much easier when one already has some experience coping with one's own. At every opportunity, we reinforce the message that your loss can help you feel for others who are also experiencing the pain of loss. In fact, this lesson may well be the greatest gift we receive in the turmoil and grief of loss.

We mention patience a lot in this book. We believe that overcoming loss is possible for everyone, but it is not possible for everyone at the same speed. Patience with grief and loss is essential to realizing wisdom and compassion. "Time heals all wounds" is the old saying, but in it there is a truth that is always new.

This book is about a serious topic, but it also has its funny parts. We believe that humor and a smile are sometimes better therapy for the pain of loss than a hundred sober, serious, and good ideas. Of course we get less humorous as the losses we describe get more serious, but at all times we have tried to lighten the heaviness of the heart with a good dose of joy. The Psalmist wrote, "Serve the Lord in joy," and we believe that joyous service is an especially good idea when things are not going well. We hope our joy always stays just this side of goofy. And whether a story we tell is serious and true or simply imagined fun, its lesson is very real.

We are both clergymen, and so references to God often appear in the book. We make no apologies for this. However, we have tried to affirm the many ways that people who are not particularly religious cope with loss. We do hope that the gentle healing God of our lives may be a source of comfort to others as well, but we know that there are many ways up the mountain.

We have also included passages from children's literature and other inspirational texts as small gifts to you between chapters. We hope they lift up in prose and verse some of the ideas that we have presented and that they will further the discussions about the mystery of loss and life that is very close to the core of our beings and at the center of our faiths.

God bless you in your losing and God bless you in your finding!

—Rabbi Marc Gellman
and Monsignor Thomas Hartman

Contents

A Word to Kids about This Book

Amazing grace! How sweet the sound
That saved a wretch like me!
I once was lost, but now am found,
Was blind, but now I see.

These are words from a famous church song.

They are also words that tell you something about this book.

Each chapter is about something you might lose in your life and also about something you might find that will help you get on with your life. That's why we called the book *Lost &*

Found. Every time something is lost, something can be found. That's the way life works here on planet Earth.

Losing stinks! You know that and we know that, but finding something that will help you get over the loss—finding something that will help you keep your hope alive, finding something that will help you get rid of your anger, finding something that will help you better understand other people—all that finding makes losing stink a little less.

You know you can't go through your life and lose *nothing.* The longer you live, the more you're going to lose. You may lose little things like toys and games, or you may lose people you love who move far away or who don't want to be your friend anymore, or maybe you will lose people because they die. We just want you to know that we believe in you and we believe that you can find something to get you through each and every loss in your life. Don't give up—and definitely don't think that what you just lost is so big that nothing can be found to help you get over it.

All of us human beings are pretty much the same. We like to win and we like to get things. But when you think about it, we learn more about life from what we lose than from what we get. In fact, finding something after you lose something you love is really the biggest gift of all.

We think God gives us that gift—but then, we always think God gives us good things.

Who knows?

You decide.

God bless you in your losing and God bless you in your finding!

—Rabbi Marc Gellman
and Monsignor Thomas Hartman

PART I

Lost, but Not Gone Forever

> *"Piglet,"* said Rabbit, taking out a pencil, and licking the end of it, *"you haven't any pluck."*
>
> *"It is hard to be brave,"* said Piglet, sniffing slightly, *"when you're only a Very Small Animal."*
>
> Rabbit, who had begun to write very busily, looked up and said:
>
> *"It is because you are a very small animal that you will be Useful in the adventure before us."*
>
> —Winnie-the-Pooh
> *A. A. Milne*

Losing Stuff

Here is a big lesson about stuff: If you have any stuff, you're definitely going to lose some of it. Some of your stuff will break and some of it will get stolen. Some will get lost and some will just wear out. Stuff is not meant to last forever, but we know that it makes you sad or angry when something you really like gets lost or busted or taken away.

We knew a kid named Flip who lost his mountain bike one day when he was riding up a mountain and a growling, drooling bear jumped out from behind a tree. When Flip turned the bike around, the bear bit his rear tire and would not let go. So Flip jumped off his bike and ran home (and told everyone the story of how he lost his bike, which of course nobody believed).

We also knew a kid named Karen who lost

her favorite doll, Murgatrude, when she was holding Murgatrude outside a car window pretending she could fly (even though her mom and dad said not to do that because if the car hit a bump, she would lose her doll—which is just exactly what happened when the car hit a big bag of french fries).

And then there was that kid named Henry who once lost his whole house with all his stuff inside when some aliens from another planet beamed Henry's house up to their spacecraft when nobody was home. People lose stuff like this all the time.

You must have your own goofy stories about stuff you lost. What was the best stuff you ever had that you ever lost? What was the funniest way you ever lost some of your stuff? Did bears or aliens ever take some of it?

It's okay to be upset about losing stuff. Some people may tell you that things don't matter. They may tell you that it's wrong to be so attached to your stuff, and that if you lose it, it's no big deal. We don't think that's true. Some things matter because they are tools.

Tools are the things you need to work or study or play. Without the right tools, you just can't do certain jobs or play certain games. If you're going to build a house, you need a saw, nails, a hammer, screws, floor plans, lumber, windows, and toilets. If you're going to play baseball, you need a baseball, a bat, bases, a playing field, chewing gum, and a hat you can put on backward. If you're going to put on the Christmas play, you need a stage and a star; a manger; costumes for three kings, a bunch of angels, Joseph, Mary, and the baby Jesus; and somebody to play a donkey. And all these things you need to build or play or act your way through life are stuff. When you lose your tools, life gets harder and definitely less fun.

Some things matter because they were presents. When somebody gives you a present, it's a sign of their love for you. Maybe the person who gave you the present had to work hard to earn enough money to buy it for you. Maybe they spent lots of time picking out just the right gift, or maybe the present is an heirloom (which means that it is some old stuff that someone in your family then passed on to you).

**When you lose your tools,
life gets harder and definitely less fun.**

Whenever you see that present, you'll think of the person who gave it to you and you'll be happy even if you don't really like it. Stuff given to you as a present is important—even if it's goofy, like the goofy ties that dads get on their birthdays or on Father's Day.

Some stuff matters just because it makes you happy—like the doll that looks so pretty, the train that makes such a wonderful whizzing sound as it goes around the tracks, the skateboard that you decorated with skulls, the model airplane that you built and flew around and around in a circle until you threw up. Stuff that makes us happy is important even if it doesn't change the world. It changes us, and that's really enough.

One thing that may help you deal with losing stuff is to remember that everybody loses things. Nobody can go through life and lose *nothing*! That just doesn't happen here on planet Earth. Stuff is just not meant to last forever. Even people don't last forever. Everybody you know has lost some stuff, and everybody you know has found something to make them feel better.

So what can *you* find when you lose stuff?

When you lose tool stuff, you can learn this

big lesson: Tools can be replaced. When a tool is lost or broken, you can get a new tool. Tools have copies because tools break and get lost all the time. Now, what if you lose a tool that you can't afford to replace? Well, then you can learn another big lesson: There are always lots of ways to do a job or play a game.

Nobody can go through life and lose NOTHING!

When you've lost a tool, think about what you need to do and how you can do it with a different tool or without that tool at all. If you lose a book, maybe the library has it. If you lose your bike, maybe you can borrow somebody else's, or walk to your friend's house, or get there on the bus. If you lose a mitt or a bat, maybe somebody at the field will lend you one (you may even make a new friend when you're asking to borrow it). Remember that the important thing about the tool is not the tool itself but what it helps you to do.

Another thing you might realize is that you don't need some stuff as much as you thought you did. It is amazing how much we have that we never use. Most people don't even remember what they got for birthdays or holidays last year! You may find that you can get on with your life just fine after you lose some things you thought you really needed.

We knew a kid named Tiffany who wore diamond earrings to kindergarten. By the time she was in high school, she refused to go to school unless her chauffeur drove her in a big white limousine. But then Tiffany's parents bought so much stuff that they didn't have any money left, and so they had to sell their house and all the diamonds and get rid of the limousine. They moved into an apartment and shared a bedroom and ate a lot of macaroni, and Tiffany was really miserable. But she didn't *have* to be miserable. You probably already know that it's more fun to eat macaroni and walk to school with your friends than to eat lobster and get driven around by some guy with a funny black hat. So when you lose your stuff, just remember that it's a lot better than being spoiled like Tiffany.

If you lose stuff that was a present, you can also find something that will help you. Of course, the first thing you'll learn is that next time you should take better care of your presents, because sometimes you don't really appreciate something until you lose it. The most important thing about a present, though, is not really the present itself but the love the person has for you that made them give you the present. You can lose the present, but you can't lose that love. Nobody can steal that love or bust it up. Nobody can sell that love in a "used love" store. Nobody can squash that love in a car-squashing machine. Nobody can throw that love off the top of a building so that it hits the ground with a big thwap! You get the idea—the present is only a sign of something larger and deeper, which can never be lost.

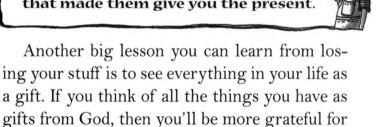

You can lose the present, but you can't lose the love the person has for you that made them give you the present.

Another big lesson you can learn from losing your stuff is to see everything in your life as a gift. If you think of all the things you have as gifts from God, then you'll be more grateful for everything you have. Your health and your life, your brain and your talents, your friends and your family—think about all of them as gifts to you from God that you might have to give back someday. If you really think about it, your life is so full of presents, you could never celebrate enough birthdays to get them all.

There is a kid named Trevor in Philadelphia who taught a lot of people just that. Trevor was watching the news one winter day and saw some poor people freezing outside in the street. He was so upset, he took off all the blankets from his bed and asked his mom to take him downtown. She did, and Trevor gave away his blankets. A rich guy saw Trevor doing this and gave him more money, right there and then, to buy more blankets for the cold people. Many people heard about how this little kid was giving away stuff and they helped him, too. Today, at Trevor's Place, poor people can come and get food or blankets or a warm safe place to sleep so that they don't have to freeze in the streets.

If you ever start *giving away* any of your stuff, we guarantee that you'll find something even bigger and more important than what you gave away. You'll find out that happiness because of stuff is good, but happiness because of people is even better. You can like stuff, but you can love people. If you try to love stuff, you'll soon find out that it can't love you back. Only people can love you back.

That's why some people who have lots of stuff can be unhappy, while other people who have almost no stuff can be very happy. The happy people have figured out that true happiness comes only from other people.

> *"What is REAL?" asked the Rabbit one day, when they were lying side by side near the nursery fender, before Nana came to tidy the room. "Does it mean having things that buzz inside you and a stick-out handle?*
>
> *"Real isn't how you are made," said the Skin Horse. "It's a thing that happens to you. When a child loves you for a long, long time, not just to play with, but REALLY loves you, then you become Real."*
>
> *"Does it hurt?" asked the Rabbit.*
>
> *"Sometimes," said the Skin Horse, for he was always truthful. "When you are Real you don't mind being hurt."*
>
> —The Velveteen Rabbit
> *Margery Williams*

Losing a Game

There is a lot of talk nowadays about being the best. Which is the best team? Who is the best player? What's the best school? Where can you get the best pizza? What is the best music? Which movie is the best? It seems that everybody is trying to buy the best or wear the best or be the best.

In sports, judges score who is the best and who is not. When you watch a game on television, you almost always see some crazy fans holding up their fingers and screaming, "We're number one!" "Best" talk hurts because it makes people who are not called "the best" feel like they're losers. They may begin to think that if they're not number one, they're number *zilch*. Once a famous football coach even told his players, "Winning isn't everything; it's the only thing!"

We think that coach was nuts.

If you think that the only thing that matters when you play a game is winning, then that game will probably not be a whole lot of fun anymore. You might yell at the umpires or coaches if you don't win; you might kick stuff or break stuff or swear a lot; you might fight with the other players. You might even cheat so that you can win. But even if you *don't* do these bad things, one bad thing will definitely happen to you: Losing won't just be hard for you; it will be painful. And you might just begin to feel that you're a general, all-around failure.

Losing is never fun, and nobody says that

you should be happy when you lose. If you play hard and do your best and really, really try to win, it hurts when you lose. Sometimes it hurts because somebody else on your team messed up and made the team lose. Sometimes losing hurts because you were the one who messed up and made the team lose. Sometimes losing hurts because you get wiped out totally. And sometimes losing hurts because you're afraid that the next time you play, maybe nobody will want to pick you for the team.

Maybe you have always been good at some game but then somebody comes along and beats you all the time. Losing when you're used to winning can be even harder to take than losing all the time.

So what can you find when you lose a game?

The big thing you have to realize when you lose is this: Nobody wins every game. Nobody wins every match. Nobody aces every test. Nobody gets every job. Nobody wins every day. Life is really more about losing than winning.

In this way, life is just like baseball. A batter who makes an out two out of every three times at bat is a great batter! A pitcher who loses four out of ten games is still a great pitcher! Even for the greatest baseball players, losing is a very common thing. In baseball and in life, the times we smack the ball over the center-field wall are few and far between. If you're going to win, you have to learn patience when you lose.

Losing helps you to learn that trying matters more than winning. Trying is what keeps you going. Trying is really the only thing you can control when you play a game or live your life. You can't decide to win, but you can decide to try to win. You can't be sure that you'll win, but you can be sure that you'll never give up.

Think of it this way: Most people learn more from losing than from winning. When you win, you might think that you did everything right, and you might think that you can sit back and relax. But losing is a wake-up call. Losing is like a cold shower. Losing makes you want to practice more, try harder, take lessons, get advice, think more clearly, and bust your butt to do better the next time.

Think of it this way: Most people learn more from losing than from winning.

The next time you lose a game, remember one other big thing that losing can teach you: It's just a game! A game is not a life-and-death struggle. A game is supposed to make you happy, not bummed out. If you find that you're miserable after you play, if you hide in your room, if you can't smile, if you kick the cat, then find a different game to play, one that makes you happy.

Losing also teaches you how to cut people some slack. When your teammate makes a bad play or loses the game for your team, why don't you go over and tell that person that everything is okay? Someday, you'll be the one making the bonehead play, and then you'll need somebody to tell you the very same thing. And if you're the kind of person who comforts others, you can bet that others will pick you up and dust you off when you're called out at home plate.

The best news is that we're always going to be picked for God's team. And even though we believe that God wants us all to do better, God still loves us just the way we are right now. It's good to know that God is always cheering for us. But God is invisible, and so we hope you have somebody in the stands you can actually see and hear clapping for you even if your team is getting wiped out that day. Everybody needs a cheerleader. Everybody needs a fan. Everybody needs to be loved, no matter what the score.

We hope that your parents love you just the same whether you win or lose, but if you have parents who scream at the refs all the time, or yell at you when you lose, or seem to love you more when you win, then it might seem that winning is more important to them than you are. If you tell your parents that you love them no matter what, and so they should love *you* no matter what, they'll probably realize that you're right. Parents are people, too, and nobody is perfect. Sometimes parents can lose sight of what matters most.

Whether you win or lose, there will always be another day and another game, another chance to learn from winning and another chance to learn from losing. Tomorrow the joy of victory and the agony of defeat will both be softened. When the day is done, knowing that you did your best is much more important than knowing that you won. In fact, knowing that you did your best is what it means to win. Then you'll never worry again about being the best.

HUG O' WAR

I will not play at tug o' war.
I'd rather play at hug o' war,
Where everyone hugs
Instead of tugs,
Where everyone giggles
And rolls on the rug,
Where everyone kisses,
And everyone grins,
And everyone cuddles,
And everyone wins.

—Where the Sidewalk Ends
Shel Silverstein

Losing a Friend

There are lots of ways to get friends, but here are some ways to lose them.

The first way to lose a friend is if a witch casts an evil spell and—*zap!*—turns your friend into a frog, and then you can't go out with your friend to a movie or a restaurant, because most restaurants and movies have big signs on the door saying quite clearly NO FROGS ALLOWED IN HERE!

But a friend can also move away from you or you can move away from a friend for lots of reasons. Your friend's family may have to move because one of the parents got a new job in another city. Maybe your friend is moving away because his or her parents are getting divorced and your friend has to live with the parent who moves away. Maybe your friend is moving because his or her family needs a bigger house, or because they want a nicer house somewhere else. Some people move away because they cannot afford to live in the same neighborhood anymore.

Even if your friend never moves, a friendship can die. Some friendships die when friends lie to each other. Some friendships die when friends betray each other by telling a secret to somebody else. Some friendships die when friends don't take time for each other or help each other out of bad spots or give support when it's really needed. Some friendships die when one friend wants the other friend to steal something or cheat or hurt somebody else and the other friend just won't do that bad thing.

Some friendships can die even when nobody does anything bad. You can start out having the same interests as your friend, and then, as you grow up, you find that you don't anymore. If your friend does not change the way you have changed, that friendship will probably die. Sometimes the stuff you do outside of school, like practicing for a sport or for the band or choir, can take up so much of your time that you don't have any left for your old friends. And sometimes friendships happen in a certain time and place, like camp.

We knew a girl named Phoebe who had a best friend from camp named Cairyn. Their favorite thing to do in camp was finding frogs along the shore of the lake. They would put them in a jar and take them back to their bunks, where they would show them to some other girls, who would scream, "Eeeeuuuu, gross!" Then Phoebe and Cairyn would laugh and laugh and let the frogs go.

Months after camp ended, Cairyn came to visit Phoebe for Thanksgiving. She started to talk about frog catching, but Phoebe was not interested. She just wanted to talk about some guy she had a crush on named Leonardo. Cairyn still liked frogs more than boys (because when you let a frog go, at least it will run away and not bother you again). Cairyn just could not get Phoebe interested in frog catching again, and Cairyn and Phoebe lost touch after that.

It's harder to be friends with somebody who lives in a different place, but it's not impossible. You can call and write and send E-mail and maybe even visit sometimes. If your friendship is really important to both of you, then you can make it work even when you're apart. Writing to a friend who has moved away is a great thing to do. It gives your friend a chance to write back to you, and old letters are a way of remembering your friend's thoughts and stories over and over again.

Another thing you can do when a friend moves away is make new friends. Not everyone thinks about reaching out to new people, but when your friend moves away, it is a chance to find new friends you might have overlooked when your old friend was still around. Take a look at all the people you never gave a chance to be your friend. New friends are one of the best ways for us to learn about new ideas and to become more open to different kinds of people. Think of how many of your close friends right now came into your life only after another good friend left you somehow. New friends are like a big present that's been sitting around patiently waiting for you to open it. Now is the time to find out what's inside.

Take a look at all the people you never gave a chance to be your friend.

In the death of a friendship, you also find out what really makes a true friend. Some people we think of as friends are not friends at all. If somebody tells your secrets or makes fun of you, or if that person always talks about herself or himself and never really asks about you, then we have got big news for you: *That person is no friend of yours!* People who do bad things to us are not our friends, no matter how much we want them to be. Learning how to spot a true friend and how to spot a false friend is one of the big lessons you can learn in life. The sooner you learn it, the more real friends you'll have.

We knew a kid named Joey who thought that

Morty was his true and real friend. They walked to school together, they played ball together at recess, and they walked home together after school. But when they passed Mr. Skrinshaw's candy and used-car store, Morty would always get Joey to go in and steal some candy to eat on the way home. Joey didn't ever really want to steal the candy, but Morty would say, "If you want me to be your friend, you better do it!"

Then one day, Morty said to Joey, "You know, if you would steal some candy *and* a car, we wouldn't have to walk home." Joey said, "What, are you nuts? I could get in real trouble." But Morty said, "If you were a *real* friend of mine, you would steal a car. You know, *real* friends stick together and do things for each other." So Joey stole a yellow Firebird with brown leather bucket seats and a screaming eagle painted on the hood. The problem with stealing a car like that is that it took the police about two seconds to find two ten-year-old kids trying to drive a Firebird. And Morty just said to the police, "Hey, Joey stole the car. Don't blame me!"

Joey found out that if you do something bad just because your friend asks you to do it, you're showing that friendship is more important than doing the right thing. But doing the right thing is always more important than keeping a friend. A true friend always helps you to choose the right thing and do the right thing and get back to doing the right thing when you go wrong. If you find yourself doing bad things, or making bad choices, or covering up bad things for your friends, get some new friends!

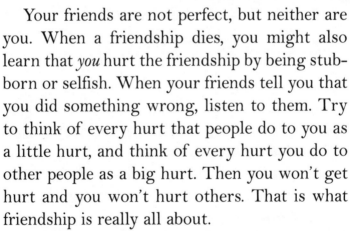

Doing the right thing is always more important than keeping a friend.

Your friends are not perfect, but neither are you. When a friendship dies, you might also learn that *you* hurt the friendship by being stubborn or selfish. When your friends tell you that you did something wrong, listen to them. Try to think of every hurt that people do to you as a little hurt, and think of every hurt you do to other people as a big hurt. Then you won't get hurt and you won't hurt others. That is what friendship is really all about.

Sometimes when we lose a friend, we learn the greatest thing of all: *Some friendships are priceless and need to be healed.* The love we have for true friends can almost always be fixed when it gets broken. Fixing friendships is one of the best and bravest, one of the hardest and happiest things we can do. When things break, things can't fix themselves. When people break, they can fix themselves with love. Love is like people glue: It sticks us back together when we break apart!

APOLOGY

It's hard to say "I'm sorry,"
Although I'm feeling sorry.
The "s" always sticks in my throat.
And "I made a big mistake"
Would produce a bellyache
That might last till I was old enough to
    vote.

"Please forgive me" sounds really good.
And I'd say it if I could,
But between the "forgive" and the
    "please"
I would have to go to bed
With a pounding in my head
And a very shaky feeling in my knees.

"I was wrong" seems oh so right.
But it gives me such a fright
That my "was" always turns into
   "ain't."
So I hope you'll take this rhyme
As my way of saying "I'm
Really sorry." Now excuse me while I
   faint.

—If I Were in Charge of the World
and Other Worries
Judith Viorst

Losing Your Health

Puking is a good thing. So is the green stuff that comes out of your nose when you sneeze, and so is the fever that sends you to bed. These are just some of the neat and gross ways your body tells you that you're sick and that you need to take care of yourself right now! Getting sick is also a kind of losing: It is losing your health.

There are a zillion ways to lose your health: You can lose your health and get sick by eating bad food or by eating too much good food. You can lose your health by running around too much or by running around too little. You can lose your health because somebody else makes you sick or because you make yourself sick. If you're too cold or too hot, if you're too fat or too thin—in fact, if you're *too* anything—there is a chance that you can lose your health.

It's no fun getting sick, even though you get to stay home from school and even though you may get some extra ice cream. When your body gets sick, it's also your mind that gets sick. You get crabby and depressed and you don't care about anything and you just want to sleep, but you can't sleep because you feel lousy and you want somebody to take away the lousy feeling inside you, but nobody can do that right away.

The worst thing about getting sick is that you can't do the things you really love to do. You can't play with your friends. You can't play

sports. You can't go out for pizza or burgers. You can't play video games. And even though you may hate going to school, staying home and missing your homework and falling behind in your class work can also be a real bummer. Getting sick and losing your health is just no fun. And sometimes it's downright scary because you don't understand what's wrong with you and when it's going to go away. Some really sick kids would tell you that they would gladly trade their best day of being sick with your worst day of being well.

After a few days or a week at most, you usually feel better and can return to your old, healthy life. Knowing that you'll get better soon and planning all of the fun things you're going to do when you get well are things you can think about when you're sick that will make you feel better even before your body is better. When you know that what you lose will be given back to you in a few days, losing it is not so bad.

But there are some kids who know that they won't get well in just a few days. These are kids who are chronically ill, which means that they're going to be sick for months or even years, and some of them will be sick for the rest of their lives. Losing your health when you know that you'll get it back very soon is no big deal, but losing your health when you know that you may never get it all back is definitely a *very* big deal.

Some really sick kids would gladly trade their best day of being sick with your worst day of being well.

We have learned a lot from chronically ill children.

Ryan was a boy with AIDS who taught us not to be afraid of sick people. When Ryan was sick, many people thought that you could get AIDS just by being in the same room with him, and he helped many people learn that this was not true. Ryan finally lost his life, but he found a way to teach people about his illness, and that gave him courage to face the pain. And Ryan gave others courage to join the fight to find a cure and to find the time and the love to care for people with AIDS instead of running away from them.

Lisa is a girl who had to wear a steel brace for five years to straighten out her spine. She taught us that there is always *something* you can do, even if your body takes a long time to

heal. Lisa could not play the sports she loved
while the brace was on, so she learned to love
to read books. She read so many books that
she got really smart, and she became a very
good writer herself. She used her "loss" to find
books.

Once you meet someone who has been sick
for a long time but is still full of hope and has
still done something great with his or her life,
it changes your own life. If those people can
still be happy after all that they have been
through, you begin to think, then why am I
complaining, when I have had so little go
wrong in my life? If getting sick for a long time
helps you to teach other people hope and
courage and love, then something really good
has come out of losing your health.

One thing everybody can learn from getting
sick is how to try to stay well. Being healthy
and staying healthy is usually not that hard. If
you eat green food, you'll be healthier than if
you eat chocolate food. If you wear a warm hat
and boots when it's below zero outside, you'll
be healthier than if you wear your favorite new
sneakers and a baseball cap. If you wash your
hands before you eat your french fries, you'll be
healthier than if you lick grimy fingers. If you

play sports, you'll be healthier than if you just play video games. If you take vitamins, you'll be healthier than if you take drugs. If you're happy and hopeful, you'll be healthier than if you're sad and scared.

> **One thing everybody can learn from getting sick is how to try to stay well.**

You know all about healthy living already. The problem is that it's easy to forget it when you're healthy. When you're healthy, you think you'll always be healthy and that you can do whatever you want and eat whatever you want. But to stay healthy, you have to work at it every day. Since there are so many things you can't control that can make you sick, it just makes sense to do all the good things you *can* control that keep you well—things like always wearing your bike helmet when you ride your bike (or when your dad or mom is practicing golf), wearing your mittens, not eating too much sugar, avoiding polar bears on the way to school, and never flying a plane without taking lessons first.

Another thing you can find when you lose

your health is prayer: You can pray to get better, and when you're well, you can remember to give thanks. Prayer will give you two big things you need when you're sick—hope to get better and courage to face your illness. Most people are born healthy and think that it is their right to be healthy, so lots of people pray to God only when they get sick. Praying when you're sick is good, but saying thanks to God when you're well is even better. It's good to learn how to pray when you need nothing! This is a good prayer to say today: "Dear God, I have enough. Thanks for everything. Please take care of the people who don't have enough. That's it. Amen."

Praying when you're sick is good, but saying thanks to God when you're well is even better.

Another good thing you can find when you lose your health is compassion. Compassion means feeling the pain of other people. Becoming a compassionate person is very important because in this world there are lots of other people and lots of pain, but there are not enough compassionate people. Mother Teresa was one of those who really could feel the pain of others. She gave homes to dying and homeless people, food to hungry people, and hope to hopeless people. She never had any children of her own, but every child she met was hers. The amazing thing about Mother Teresa was not that she could feel for one sick person but that she could feel compassion for thousands of sick people, one person at a time. She showed the whole world that being surrounded by poor, sick people does not have to make you hard. Her work with the poorest of the poor on this planet made her soft.

The only way the world is going to get better is if people who have what they need learn to help people who don't have enough of what they need. Here's the deal: In your life, you're going to meet people who need help. If you can help them, you *should* help them. Learning how to help people who are sick is a *huge* good thing that you could learn from the bad thing of being sick. So you see, the world is waiting for you!

Now, isn't fixing the world worth a little puke or some green stuff coming out of your nose?

One strange thing about Being In A Crisis, especially being at the center of one, is how everything else just keeps moving along. You don't think it will. You don't see how it can. When Dr. Conner stood at the side of my bed and delivered her news, it felt like every other part of the world should have reacted to what had just happened in mine. The nurses should have paused, traffic in the streets should've pulled over, babies should've stopped crying. Just for a minute, just to acknowledge that for some reason, my life had changed. But nobody seemed to notice. Even Dr. Conner. She dropped her bomb, nodded at us, and left. And the day went on.

We crashed, me and my parents and my Sam. Then we went on, too. That's the other thing about A Crisis. When you're outside of it, not touched by it, you say, "Oh, my God, how do they stand it? Poor things, how could they live through that?" When it's around you, in you, you simply do it. Because there's no choice. Only a next step.

—A Time for Dancing
Davida Wills Hurwin

Losing Your Brothers and Sisters When They Leave Home

We know that there are days when you *want* your brothers and sisters to move away to the city on planet Earth that is as far away from your house as it can be. On the days they tease you, on the days they borrow your clothes without asking, on the days they spend too much time in the bathroom when you really have to use it, on the days they get you in trouble with your parents, on the days when they hog the telephone, on the days when they scare you and your friends, on *those* days your brothers and sisters may seem like a huge pain in the butt.

But on lots of other days, you'll remember that the love you have for your siblings (which means your brothers or sisters) is so very deep and so very special that there is really nothing like it in the world. Your siblings can teach you stuff that you would have to learn the hard way if it weren't for them. They can tell you things about how to get a date or how to dress or how to stick up for yourself or how to get out of a jam, and what they tell you is stuff you'll never hear from your mom or dad. In fact, there is a really good chance that your brother or your sister might turn out to be your very best friend. Having a brother or a sister is one of the best things in the whole wide world, and even if you don't feel lucky now, you'll feel lucky someday.

The love you have for your siblings is so very special that there is really nothing like it in the world.

The deep and special love you have for your brothers and sisters is exactly why losing them is so hard. You want your brothers and sisters to live near you (with their own bathroom), but what will probably happen is that sometime in your life your brothers and sisters will move away from you, at least for a few years.

Your brothers and sisters may move out when they go to college. They may leave to get a job. They may leave to get married and move

into their own home. They may move out to go
into the army. They may move to the South
Pole to follow the penguins around and see
what they do when they're not catching fish.
Even if you are going to get their old bedroom
or phone when they move, it is a hard thing to
know, when you go into their bedroom to ask
their opinion on your clothes or haircut, that
they'll not always be there.

When you lose brothers and sisters because
they go to college, you can still see them quite
a bit. They'll come home for vacations. They
might come home to get their laundry washed,

and they'll come home to get some good food and some more money. If they're moving out of your town for good and if you have a phone (or a piece of paper, an envelope, and a stamp, or a computer with E-mail), you can talk to them and share your life with them just the way you did when they were living at home.

You may actually find that writing to your siblings is even better in some ways than talking to them and shouting at them through the bathroom door the way you did when they were at home. You're not competing for the TV or for the best grades in school or for your parents' attention. When you write a letter, you think more about what you really want to say, which is usually a lot nicer than what you would say to them at home. It is especially fun to read what they write back to you, and you may get along better and love them more deeply than you have in years.

When your brothers and sisters move away to get married, it can be hard, because instead of spending their time talking to you, they're mostly talking to their new husbands or wives. It can also be weird because they're bringing new people into your family. This can change some things in the way your family works. You have to make other places at the table for family dinners. You have more presents to buy during the holidays, and you have other people who need to use the bathroom when you really want to get in.

The good thing you can find when you lose your brothers and sisters is how it feels to grow up. Sometimes it is hard to grow up, to see your family change, to let go of your childhood, to accept the way life changes. But you don't want to be a little kid sister or brother all your life. You don't want to go to school your whole life. You don't want to share a bathroom your whole life. And best of all, you begin to see that you don't really need your brother's or sister's advice about everything and you don't really need someone to protect you from the bullies at school. You can take care of yourself.

**But you don't want to be
a little kid sister or brother
all your life.**

As you grow up, you'll find new and deep ways to stay connected to your brothers and sisters. The only thing that really changes is where you guys sleep. The love you have for each other does not have to change. One thing we learned from the love we have for our own brothers and sisters (Judy, Joanne, Larry, Sheila, Joanne, Jerry, Eileen, and John) is that moving away from one another made our love *stronger*. Nothing can make it go away unless they get beamed up to some alien spaceship and are taken to a planet with no pay phones—which happens, but not that often. Love will always find a way to call you back because families are the best and strongest places where we each find love.

> *The organist started "Here Comes the Bride" and we all turned to the back of the church, expectant, and there she was. My father was grinning, his arm linked with hers as they took the first step together. Everyone was oohing and aahing because she was beautiful, white and gliding and perfect, and I watched her come towards me, a small smile on her face. I saw Lewis blushing and my mother dabbing her eyes and I thought about all we'd been through, my sister and I, the fights and the good times and every day we'd had that led up to this one*

and suddenly I was crying. I knew my mascara was running and I was the only one up there in front so close to bawling, but still the tears came, rolling down my cheeks as she got closer and her own eyes met mine from beneath her veil. I wanted to say it all then, but before I could speak she stepped away from my father and put her arms around me, hugging me tightly, her bouquet against my neck. I smelled flowers, my mother's garden, as I held her and knew I didn't have to say anything. My sister was wiser than I ever gave her credit for. She held me and whispered she loved me before pulling back, wiping her own eyes.

—That Summer
Sarah Dessen

Losing Your Mom or Dad in a Divorce

Losing brothers or sisters when they move out of your house can be bad, but there is no way that it is as bad as when your mom or dad moves out of the house because your parents are getting divorced. Dealing with a divorce in your family can sometimes be as hard as dealing with a death in your family. A death is final—you're very sad, but then you learn to move on. In a divorce, the arguing between your parents and with other members of your family could go on for years. This can make everybody in the family miserable, and on top of that, a lot of big changes can happen in your life.

You may be left living with one parent for part of the time and with another parent for another part of the time. You may have two bedrooms in two separate homes, two sets of clothes, two desks, and two toothbrushes. If your mom and dad get remarried, you may also find that you have two more parents and maybe even some new brothers and sisters to boot. There is no doubt about it: Divorce is tough. It is losing your family the way it *used* to be.

One of the hardest things for kids in a divorce is trying not to take sides. Maybe one or both of your parents will want you to take sides, but you need to be able to deal with both of them. You may need to learn how not to get trapped in the middle of their fights, and how not to blame them for getting divorced. It's not easy, but you *can* do this for one big reason: Your mom is your dad's ex-wife and your dad is your mom's ex-husband, but you're *not* their ex-child. They both still love you, and you can find a way to love both of them.

We knew a kid named Alon who thought his parents got divorced because they could not agree on how to cut cheese. Alon's dad liked to cut the cheese in thin slices, but Alon's mom liked to cut the cheese in chunks. So Alon learned how to cut cheese in chunks when he was eating with his mom, and he learned how to cut cheese in slices when he was with his dad. For a long time, Alon thought that his folks were getting divorced because of the cheese.

Only later did he realize that the fights about how to cut the cheese were just a little sign that there were bigger problems in his parents' marriage.

No one gets divorced for silly little reasons. Lots of parents argue and yell and learn how to work things out. Just because you hear your parents arguing doesn't mean they're getting divorced. If your folks *do* get divorced, it will be for a big reason. And then you'll have plenty of time to figure out how each of them likes to cut the cheese!

You also need to know that you're not in

charge of taking care of your parents' problems. Most kids can hardly fix their spelling, so it's just silly to think that kids can fix a marriage. Many marriages can be fixed, but people need marriage counselors, who help husbands and wives with marriage therapy. We hope that every couple tries their very best to fix their marriage before they ever agree to get divorced. It is always a sad thing when a marriage is lost, and it is a *very* sad thing when a marriage is lost that was waiting to be found. But your parents are the *only* ones who can "find" it.

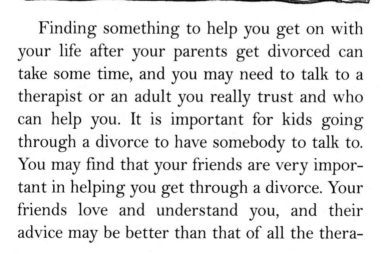

You're not in charge of taking care of your parents' problems.

Finding something to help you get on with your life after your parents get divorced can take some time, and you may need to talk to a therapist or an adult you really trust and who can help you. It is important for kids going through a divorce to have somebody to talk to. You may find that your friends are very important in helping you get through a divorce. Your friends love and understand you, and their advice may be better than that of all the therapists in the world, especially if some of your friends have already been in your shoes. Also, you might have a special person in your family, maybe an uncle or an aunt or a cousin or even a brother or a sister who can be a big help to you if you'll only reach out. As long as you're loved, you're never alone.

There are actually a few good things that some kids have found after their parents divorce. One is that kids might see their mom and dad happy for the first time. It's very hard to live in a marriage that has little love in it, and after a divorce your mom and dad may finally have a chance to find a healthier love and be happy.

After a divorce, you may be able to see your mom and dad as real human beings for the first time. Lots of kids think that their moms and dads are perfect, but when we grow up, we learn that nobody is perfect, not even our parents. When you begin to see their weaker parts, you'll also begin to better see their wonderful parts. After a divorce, you may find a way to love the good things in your mom and dad, and to forgive them for the things that are hard to accept. It's sort of like when you eat an orange. You don't eat the whole thing—you eat the sweet part and throw away the bitter skin. You need to know how to take the sweet parts of people and leave behind the parts that make your face squinch up.

After a divorce, you may be able to see your mom and dad as real human beings for the first time.

After a divorce, you may also find that you're more independent than you have ever been before, and you may learn that you can take care of yourself better than you ever thought you could. You'll still be taken care of by your mom and dad, but there will probably be only one parent around at a time. If that parent can't be around you every minute, you'll need to be able to take care of yourself. Everybody has to learn that in growing up, but sometimes divorce makes you learn it a little faster and a little earlier.

Growing up is a good thing. Even getting married is a good thing. Some kids who grow up in homes where there was a divorce are afraid to get married when they grow up. But marriage is the way we get out of our skin and into the skin of somebody else. Marriage is the way we find somebody to share our soul and our life, our love and our children. Marriage gives us the way to make a family, the place to live our life in the deepest way, and the courage to be tender. Marriage is a risk, but anything that does all these great things is worth it.

> *You gain strength, courage and confidence by every experience in which you really stop to look fear in the face. You are able to say to yourself, "I lived through this horror. I can take the next thing that comes along.". . . You must do the thing you think you cannot do.*
>
> —You Learn by Living
> *Eleanor Roosevelt*

Losing a Part of Your Body

Every part of our bodies has a purpose. Legs are for walking and for having something to put into your pant legs. Noses are for smelling and for holding up glasses. Butts are for giving you something to sit on. Eyebrows are for keeping bugs from falling into your eyes. Fingers are for grabbing cookies, and your appendix is for something, but we have no idea what that something is. Every part of your body is there for a reason, and so when you lose a part of your body, or when you were born without a part of it, that's a very big loss.

When people see somebody with a missing part, sometimes they don't know what to do. Should they pretend not to notice the missing part, they wonder, or should they say something about it? So if it is *you* who has a missing part, the best thing to do is show people that you're comfortable with yourself. Then the people you meet will feel comfortable with you.

How do you get comfortable with yourself if you have lost a part of your body? One way is to understand that you are not your body. Your body is kind of like a case for your soul, which is what you're *really* like. And even though you may have lost *some* parts of your body, you still have lots of parts left. By learning how to make your other parts stronger, you can overcome the loss of the parts you don't have. Have you ever seen the shoulder muscles of the people who use wheelchairs? Their shoulder muscles are usually stronger than those of people who have legs.

You are not your body. Your body is kind of like a case for your soul, which is what you're REALLY like.

We knew a guy named Dennis who lost his leg in an automobile accident and was about to give up on his life. Then he saw the Special Olympics on television and he saw a guy running really fast with an artificial leg. So Dennis decided to become the fastest runner with one leg in the world. He practiced and practiced, and after a few years he won the gold medal at the Special Olympics. With an artificial right leg, he ran the one-hundred-meter race only about two seconds slower than the record time of the runner with two real legs!

Todd was a fifteen-year-old boy who had lost his left leg to cancer. Todd also wanted to give up until he saw the Special Olympics, and he began to train to run the four-hundred-meter race. One day, Todd and Dennis met, and they decided that it was not enough for them just to run in races. They decided to visit schools and talk to children. They gave hope to many who had lost a part of their bodies, but they also talked to kids who had all their parts and gave them a chance to see what a leg stump and an artificial leg look like, so that they wouldn't be afraid of kids who are different.

What is normal anyway? People come in lots of different shapes and sizes and with lots of missing parts, and they all can make terrific lives out of what they have been given. Pennies are all the same, and so are nickels and quarters and dollar bills, and computer chips and decks of cards and baseballs, but people are all different, and that is the great thing about people. From every person, we can learn something and in every person we can see something beautiful and fine. God really gave us all much more than we need to live, and we can lose some of our parts and still live a great life.

Steven was a young policeman who was shot in the spine. Afterward, he could not move his arms or legs. Everybody who knew Steven thought that he would just want to die, because he loved his job and he loved to play sports. And so it really amazed people when Steven forgave the guy who shot him. He taught other people who can't move their arms or legs how to live

with their loss. He said that as long as we're alive, we have something to be grateful to God for, and it does not matter what we can't do. All that matters is what we *can* do. One of the things Steven can do best is hug his son Connor: Connor climbs onto his father's lap and then Steven kind of nuzzles Connor with his face. It is one of the greatest kinds of hugs we have ever seen.

There's a guy named Christopher Reeve who played Superman in the movies. Then he was paralyzed after falling off a horse. Instead of being depressed and angry, he talked to kids about what it was like to be paralyzed and how there is always something good to do, no matter how much you can't do. His courage gave courage to many people, and now he really *is* a superman.

Losing your sight or your hearing is very hard because most of what we learn about the world comes to us through our eyes or our ears. Being deaf or blind can be a big loss, but we know many blind and deaf people who have done wonderful things with their lives. We know a man named Richard who became a United States federal judge when he was visually impaired. Nobody thought that he could do the work, but he worked hard and never gave up. He has a guide dog named Coach who helps him get around. When you're visually impaired, it is a good thing to have an animal friend lick your face and remind you that you're going to get to the place God wants you to go, no matter how hard the journey. If you have people or animals who love you in your life, you'll be just fine no matter how many parts you're missing. The one thing you can't afford to lose is love.

You may know about the life of Helen Keller, who was deaf and blind at a time when there were not that many people who were willing to help. In her day, blind and deaf people were treated like animals. But Helen Keller's teacher, a great woman named Annie Sullivan, taught Helen how to communicate. Her teaching and Helen's courage and patience taught the world that hearing- or visually impaired people were not helpless and hopeless. Reading books about Helen Keller or other people who have gotten through hard times might help you to get through the hard times you face in your own life.

If you're missing a part of your body, you'll also find out just how many people really do care about people like you and want to help. You'll meet teachers and physical therapists; you'll meet coaches and doctors and nurses and other parents who all want to help you lead a rich and full life. They're just like Annie Sullivan. We think of them as angels God has sent to take care of all the people who just need a different kind of help to get through life.

For medical help, people without certain parts are living in the best of times, and things are only getting better. Scientists can use computers and new plastics and metals to make copies of the parts you might be missing. Once, people without legs had to walk with wooden crutches. Now many of them can have prostheses made, which means replacement parts for your body. People can work at computers even if they can't move their hands. People can talk over the Internet even if they don't have a tongue. People can see with Braille even if they have no eyes. The chances are that if you're missing a part, there is some teacher or tool that will help you get around in the world.

We know a guy who was born with no legs. His name is Henry Viscardi. His dad was so ashamed of having a son with no legs that he would not take Henry home from the hospital for a long time; then he put Henry in other hospitals just so that he would not have to look at his son. Finally, Henry's mother got his father to let him come home. Henry grew up to be a great person. In fact, Henry was the guy who made America sit up and take notice of people with disabilities. Most of the laws that help people who use wheelchairs came from Henry Viscardi's fight for the rights of these people. What Henry Viscardi found was pride and courage. If he had been born with legs, maybe Henry would not have done so much with his life. Who knows?

We heard a story about a prince who had a perfect shiny ruby given to him by his father, the king. Every year on his birthday, he would take the big ruby out of its box and look at it. Then one year, the prince dropped the box and the ruby fell out and was badly scratched. He called all his experts to ask them if they could fix it, but none of the experts could remove the scratch. Then the daughter of one of his servants came forward and told the sad prince that she could fix the ruby. Nobody had a better idea, so the prince gave it to her. After a few days, the girl returned to the prince and showed him the ruby. The prince smiled a big smile, and everyone gathered around the girl to see: She had used the scratch as the stem of a beautiful rose that she had etched into the precious stone. In gratitude, the prince gave the ruby to the little girl to keep. So you see, there is always a rose waiting to grow around every single scratch you get in your life.

Now, losing a part of your body is more than just a scratch, but there is nothing that you lose that cannot be a part of some new and beautiful design for your life. You know, everybody is missing something. Nobody has all their parts all the time. Some people are missing kindness. Some are missing the part that makes them honest. Some are missing the part that helps them be happy.

Nobody is perfectly whole.

Everybody needs help.

> *Dear Dexter:*
>
> *I got your letter. Thanks for writing it. I'm sitting on the beach at one of my favorite places. For a long time I thought I'd never be able to come here ever again, but maybe even when you're in a wheelchair you can still decide to do whatever you want to do.*
>
> *Yes, I knew you were on the same floor I was. I knew you came by my room once, too. I always wondered why you didn't come in. I guess I didn't stop to*

think about how the accident was for you. I was so sure it had happened only to me.

Maybe it'll make you feel better to know what I'm going to do two weeks from now. I'm going to enter a wheelchair race. A friend of mine named Harris got me the entry forms, and he's been helping me train for it.

For a long time I didn't think I ever wanted to see you again, but if you ever come back to Hudson to visit your mom, why don't you come by? Maybe it'd make both of us feel better if we could talk about what happened.

But that's over. We've both got to get used to how our lives are now. Thanks again for writing to me, Dexter. Good luck to you too.

> *Your friend,*
> *Megan (the Magnificent)*

Megan folded the letter just as Harris and Joey came back. . . . She smiled up at them. Funny; she'd never realized letting go would feel so good.

—Picking Up the Pieces
Patricia Calvert

Losing Confidence

Michael Jordan always wants the ball. Even when he misses, he still wants the ball. Even when he *retires*, the guy will still want the ball.

Michael Jordan has confidence. He believes that he'll make the shot and score the winning basket. He's a big success not only because he's good at playing basketball but also because he believes in himself. Now, you're not Michael Jordan, but you don't have to be Mike to be like Mike. You can learn how to want the ball, too. You can learn how to find confidence even if you have lost it.

There are lots of ways people lose confidence.

A guy named Furdy was really good at doing stuff with computers. Furdy could program them and get into the secret parts of other computers that he wasn't supposed to get into. One day, Furdy got into a part of a secret military computer. Then some guys with guns and badges and sunglasses found out and came to Furdy's house. They yelled at him for a long time and told him that what he had done was a big crime and also very stupid and that he could go to jail for the rest of his life. Getting yelled at by guys with guns and badges and sunglasses can make anybody lose confidence.

Elsie lost her confidence when she was elected class president and she said she would get a french-fry machine and ice cream put into the lunchroom, but when she did it, the french fryer caught fire and melted all the ice cream and set off the sprinklers, which soaked all her friends, who blamed Elsie and so nobody would talk to her. When people won't talk to you, it's easy to lose your confidence.

Biff lost his confidence because people thought he had a really big butt. Biff needed two chairs to hold just one butt. Kids were always making fun of Biff, and soon he grew ashamed of his body. Being ashamed of your body is another way you can lose your confidence.

Maybe it's how you look, maybe it's how you talk, maybe it's what you believe, or maybe it's what you do—whatever it is, losing confidence

in yourself makes you not want the ball anymore, and if you don't want the ball, you can
never play the game!

The first step to finding your confidence
again after you lose it is to understand that
there is nothing wrong with you. Being embarrassed is okay, but being ashamed is not okay.
We all get embarrassed sometimes. Maybe your
pants fell down during the school play, or
maybe you puked on the school trip, or maybe
you had a big zit on your nose the day of the
school dance. But when you're ashamed, you
don't just think that something bad happened *to*

you. You think that something is bad *about* you. Being embarrassed is like getting mud on your clothes, and being ashamed is more like getting a stain. It's easy to get mud off, but it's much harder to get the stain out. Sometimes a stain can even leave a permanent mark.

To keep your confidence (or find it after you lose it), you have to know what you're good at. When you're young and just trying stuff out, you're going to have lots of screwups. This is normal and it's all a part of trying to find the thing that God gave you the ability to do really well. The whole point of the early part of your life is to keep trying new things until you find one you do well. It really is so simple: The things you'll be happiest doing are things you're good at doing. The most unhappy people are the ones who don't even bother to try to fig- ure it out. It may take a long time, but it's worth the search.

Amy always wanted to bake bread, but her parents told her that she should be a lawyer. When she became a lawyer, she had no confi- dence and hated it every day, until she quit to start her own bread-baking company. It was a terrific success because Amy always had the confidence that she could bake the best bread in the world. Finally she was happy because she was doing what she had always loved to do.

Another way to find confidence is to try not to envy what other people can do. If you watch Michael Jordon and say, "I could never do that," and get depressed because of it, it will be even harder to discover what you can do that Mike can't do. You can even be happy when you see somebody else doing something great. Just think of it as inspiration for becoming great yourself. Or think of it as a chance to see God's gifts in somebody else.

One way to get your confidence back if you have lost it is to try very hard just to ignore what others think about you. If you worry too much about what other people think about you, then you'll never figure out what *you* think about you.

Did you know that some of the greatest human discoveries and creations would never have been made if the people behind them had cared about what other people thought of their work? Einstein flunked out of high school. Beethoven's piano teacher said that he had no talent. Thomas Edison's teachers told his parents that Thomas was too dumb to do anything with his life. Walt Disney was fired by a news-

paper editor who said that he had no good ideas.
The father of the famous sculptor Rodin said, "I
have an idiot for a son." Abraham Lincoln failed
in two businesses he started, had a nervous
breakdown, was rejected from law school, and
lost four jobs and eight elections before he
became maybe the greatest president of the
United States. A lot of people were wrong
about those geniuses, and all the people who
make you lose your confidence are wrong, too!

**Some of the greatest discoveries
would never have been made if the people
behind them had cared about what other
people thought of their work.**

Another way to gain confidence is to practice
your butt off. When Michael Jordan was in high
school, he had talent but no confidence. In fact,
he could not even make his high school basketball team! So one day Mike decided to practice
really hard on his game, and the rest is history.
In fact, Mike still practices very hard, even
though he's a big star. People say that being a
success is 10 percent inspiration and 90 percent
perspiration. This means that working hard to
develop your talents is the only way you'll get

good at anything, no matter how big your talents are.

Another thing you can do to boost your confidence is to hang out with people who believe in you. If you're always around people who treat you like you're worthless, you're going to feel worthless. Look for friends who believe in you, or teachers who believe in you, or members of your family who believe in you, or coaches who believe in you, or priests, rabbis, ministers, or imams who believe in you. And even more important: These people should not focus on whether you succeed or fail.

One more thing to remember is that God always believes in you. No matter what other people tell you, you must always believe that God knows you're terrific. Among all the people who ever were and who ever will be, God never made anybody just like you. You're special and wonderful and God gave you blessings that God gave to nobody else in the whole wide world.

So get ready! Here comes the ball!

All your life you are told the things you cannot do. All your life they will say you are not good enough or strong enough or talented enough, they will say you're the wrong height or the wrong weight or the wrong type to play this or be this or achieve this.

THEY WILL TELL YOU NO.

A thousand times no until all the no's become meaningless. All your life they will tell you no, quite firmly and very quickly. They will tell you no, and

YOU WILL TELL THEM YES.

—Anonymous

Losing Trust

You know how it happens. Your parents promise to do something for you and then they don't
do it. So they say, "We didn't really promise; we
just said we would *try* to do it." Or, if they
really did promise, they might say, "Okay, we
promised, but we can't do it for you right now
because something has come up." Or maybe
they don't say anything at all and then you hit
them with "I am *never* going to trust you again!"

Well, of course, when your anger goes away,
you do trust your parents again, and most of
the time when they promise you something,
they do deliver. Parents don't charge us rent
and usually don't make us buy the groceries.
We all know that just because they don't come
through with our full Christmas list does not
mean that they don't love us or should not be
trusted. There *are* people in this world you

should never trust, but mostly these people are not your parents!

Some kids lose trust because the stuff they get doesn't work the way it was supposed to work. When the space cadet intergalactic discombobulator that you saw advertised on television that shot laser beams into an alien cave fortress and blew up its framitz incendiater turns out to be a cheap plastic gun with a flashlight inside, it's easy to lose trust in things. This happened to a kid we knew named Herbert. He was crushed, and he never trusted anything he bought anywhere ever again. (He would even open the cereal boxes in the supermarket to see if there really was cereal inside and peel bananas to see if there really were bananas inside the skin!)

If you lose trust in stuff, you can get trust again by remembering a few things. Trusting people always makes more sense than trusting things. Things can't love us. Things can't stick up for us. Things can't even hug us or kiss us or tell us that everything is going to be okay. So when your space cadet intergalactic discombobulator fizzles, just say to yourself, "It was only a thing that fizzled, not a person who cares."

But trusting people doesn't always work out.

Sometimes you lose trust because a person you trusted has betrayed you. Maybe the person told a secret that he or she was supposed to keep. Maybe the person promised to invite you to a party but then never did. Maybe the person didn't stick up for you when other kids were saying bad things about you. Being hurt by one person you trust can make you start to lose trust in all people.

Jenifah lost trust in all her friends because she told Jaymie to keep a secret about how Jordan had kissed her with his mouth open behind the skating house. Jaymie then went right over and told Jordan's best friend, J.B.,

who told Suzi, who told Nedra, who told Mrs. Snouder, who teaches the health class—who then talked about how if you kiss with your mouth open, you can get trillions of germs from the person you're kissing and how it's just like swallowing their spit (and all the time Mrs. Snouder was looking at Jordan and Jenifah). Jenifah was so embarrassed by the whole thing that she never trusted any of her friends again.

Some kids lose trust when the world lets them down. If you watch the news, you may think that everybody in the world is in a car or plane crash, or a fire or flood, or is getting murdered. With all of the bad news you see every day on TV and in the papers, you can easily believe that goodness will never win over evil, that happiness will never win over sadness, and that life will never win over death. This can make you lose trust in people, in the world, and even in God.

This happened to Shaniqua, who saw on TV how little snail darters were going to be killed by a new dam that would flood out the shallow-water wetlands where these fish lived. So Shaniqua painted a sign: SAVE THE SNAIL DARTERS! THEY'RE REALLY CUTE FISH! Then she took the sign and her blanket and mattress and put them right near the river where they were going to build the dam. This stopped the bulldozers. But when the people building the dam told her that even though the snail darters were cute, they had to build the dam anyway, Shaniqua said, "It's just not fair. The world stinks! I give up!" And she sat on a rock and cried. But a guy took her picture, which appeared in the papers. Then the TV people wanted to interview her, and then everybody wrote letters to help Shaniqua—and it worked! The dam was stopped and the snail darters were saved. Shaniqua never believed that anything was impossible ever again. We hope you all have the chance to see people come through for you, like Shaniqua did.

With all of the bad news you see every day, you can easily believe that goodness will never win over evil.

When you lose trust, it is like a tree getting pulled out of the ground. If you want the tree to live, you have to plant it again. When you lose trust, you need to find a way to get trust back in your life again if you ever want to be happy.

The ways you can find trust depend on the ways you lost it.

If you lose your trust because a person lets you down, you can still rebuild your trust in people by going to somebody who never let you down and talking about it. The trust you have for some people is like a rock. It will never go away and it will never be broken. Being with somebody you still trust will help you remember that not *all* people are jerks!

Learning whom to trust is one of the hardest and biggest lessons in life. Life is filled with good and kind people who want to help you, but there are always a few people you should never trust, because they just want to hurt you, or cheat you, or use you to get what they want. Sometimes you're going to guess wrong about whom to trust. This happens to everybody, even the smartest people.

One day, a guy named Chuckie went to Mikey (a really brainy guy and the president of a big company) and sold him an automatic toothbrush and face washer (you just put your face in a helmet and it shot soapy water onto your face and toothpaste into your mouth). When Mikey tried it for the first time, it brushed his face and washed his teeth, and it kept going until it had brushed off his eyebrows and most of his nose hair. So being smart is no insurance policy against being scammed by some guy with an automatic toothbrush and face-washing helmet to sell you.

Learning whom to trust is one of the hardest and biggest lessons in life.

When something like that happens, just pick yourself up and move on with your life a little more carefully. Life is filled with little and big hurts, and each hurt makes you wiser and stronger and more grown-up. Remember, our bumps are what make us who we are.

Maybe losing trust in people will teach you not to expect perfection from the people in your life. Nobody can keep all their promises—not even parents—so cut them some slack! If the person who promised you something did everything that he or she could do to fulfill the promise but couldn't do it, you're a lucky person. The Scottish poet Robert Burns wrote, "The best laid schemes o' mice and men / Gang aft a-gley; / An' lea'e us nought but grief and pain, / For promis'd joy." This means that no matter how well you plan, things mess up. Learning not to expect so much may make it easier for you to trust, because you won't be keeping score.

But what do you do if the whole *world* lets you down? Helping one person at a time is the best way we know not to get depressed about the evil and hardship in the world. If you think about all of the badness on Earth, you'll never be able to bring any goodness, but if you just take care of that one person who is in front of you and who needs help from you, then everything will be all right. That's really how the world will be changed—one person at a time.

Anne Frank was a Jewish girl who lived in hiding from the Nazis during World War II. In her diary, she wrote:

It's twice as hard for us young ones to hold our ground, and maintain our opinions, in a time when all ideals are being shattered and destroyed, when people are showing their worst side, and do not know whether to believe in truth and right and in God. . . .

It's really a wonder that I haven't dropped all my ideals, because they seem so absurd and impossible to carry out. Yet I keep them, because in spite of everything I still believe that people are really good at heart.

I simply can't build up my hopes on a foundation consisting of confusion, misery, and death. . . . I can feel the sufferings of millions and yet, if I look up into the heavens, I think that it will all come right, that this cruelty too will end, and that peace and tranquility will return again. . . .

—Anne Frank: The Diary of a Young Girl
Anne Frank

PART II

When Good-bye Is Forever:
Losing Because of Death

In death, two worlds meet with a kiss: the world going out and the future coming in.

—The Jerusalem Talmud

The Big Things about Death

It would be just great if nobody we loved ever died. Then we wouldn't have to face death or think about it or be scared about it. We hope that you have not had to think about death at all in your life up to now. You should spend most of your time thinking about life and about all the great things that have been put into your life. But everybody has to think about death *sometime*. Here are five big things we have learned about death that have given us comfort. Maybe they will help you, too.

Death Is Forever

Losing because of death is the hardest way to lose, because in many ways death is forever.

When you lose your brother to college, or

your friend to another town, or your parent to
a divorce, they're not in your life the same way
as before, but they're still in it! When people
you love die, you won't be able to see them,
kiss them, sing with them, bake cookies with
them, go sledding with them, or just take a
walk with them. That's what makes death so
scary to so many people. Death is a permanent
loss. That is why it is so tough to find something good after death that will help you go on
with your life.

It's hard to understand the idea of forever.
When you tell a little kid that Grandpa died,
sometimes he or she thinks that Grandpa just
went to Florida again for the winter and will
be back in the spring. But forever means forever
and ever. And nothing except death is forever.
Life is not forever. Being a kid is not forever.
Having to wait to use the bathroom is not forever. Death is really the only forever thing we
face in life.

But most religious people believe that death
is *not exactly* forever. Most every religion
teaches that it is only our bodies that die, not
our souls. Our souls are a little piece of God in
us. Souls are kind of like God's telephone to

our best part. They help God keep in touch with us and remind us to do the right thing. Our souls are not in us the way our tonsils are in us or the way our stomach is in us or the way that green stuff in our nose is in us. Most parts of us can be yanked out of us by a doctor, but a doctor can't ever yank out a person's soul, because souls are invisible.

Death is really the only forever thing we face in life.

God is invisible, so our souls must be invisible, too. It's not that hard to understand how something invisible can be real. Think of the love your mom or dad has for you. That love is invisible, but it's real. Well, the soul is the way God's love comes into us, so it just makes sense that it would be invisible, too.

The place our souls go after death is called "heaven" by some religions. Some religions call it the "world to come" and some call it "paradise" or other names, but the idea is the same. The idea is that death is forever for your body but not for your soul. We're both religious guys and we believe that God's love for all of us is so deep that it is stronger than death. We believe that the souls of all those you love who died are in heaven with God, who is taking care of them even better than they took care of you.

We believe that their souls *can* touch you and watch over you and protect you for the rest of your life. The really neat thing about heaven is that even though the souls of the people you love are there, you can feel them here. You can feel their love for you and their protection of you right here on Earth. You may feel their souls coming near to you at certain times of your life. When you're sitting around the Christmas tree or at a holiday meal or when you're just in your room wishing that they were near, you may get a warm feeling that they're right there in the room with you. We don't believe that they can talk to you or that you can talk to them, but we do believe that their love for you will never ever leave you, even if you don't believe in heaven. If you're not sure what you believe, that's okay. You don't need to believe in heaven to get there (it's just that if you don't believe in heaven and you *do* get there, you're going to be *really* surprised).

Dear Editor: I am 8 years old.

Some of my little friends say there is no Santa Claus.

Papa says "If you see it in The Sun *it's so."*

Please tell me the truth; is there a Santa Claus?

Virginia O'Hanlon

Virginia,

Your little friends are wrong. . . . They do not believe except [what] they see. . . .

Yes, Virginia, there is a Santa Claus. He exists as certainly as love and generosity and devotion exist, and you know that they abound and give to your life its highest beauty and joy. Alas! how dreary would be the world if there were no Santa Claus! . . . We should have no enjoyment, except in sense and sight. . . .

Nobody sees Santa Claus, but that is no sign that there is no Santa Claus. The most real things in the world are those that neither children nor men can see.

—The New York Sun, *September 21, 1897*

Death Comes to Everyone

We all know that everybody who lives will die someday, but it's hard to believe it. We get used to the people we love being in our life today, and we never think that they won't be with us tomorrow. Well, on some tomorrow, they'll be gone. If we were angels, we would never die, but if we were angels, we also would never be able to play soccer or eat a hot fudge sundae or kiss our grandmas. Being a person means that we get all the good parts and all the bad parts of life.

You don't need to be scared, because everybody dies. Knowing that everybody dies is one of the best ways we're connected to one another. Everybody alive thinks about dying and about the people they love dying, just like you do. It is comforting to know that we're all in the same boat. We're all trying to get through life happy and kind and loving, and if you spend your time worrying about dying, you can't ever be happy.

Life for most people is good and long and full of great stuff. We can't decide how many days we have, but we can decide how full each day will be. Think of each day as a great gift, a special present from God. You have been given another day! Now go out there and enjoy it and do something good in it and learn something important in it, because you just never know how many days you'll get. Right now, your life needs you. Death will take care of itself!

MY OWN DAY

When I opened my eyes this morning,
The day belonged to me.
The sky was mine and the sun,
And my feet got up dancing.
The marmalade was mine and the
  squares of sidewalk
And all the birds in the trees.
So I stood and I considered
Stopping the world right there,
Making today go on and on forever.
But I decided not to.
I let the world spin on and I went to
  school.
I almost did it, but then, I said to myself,
"Who knows what you might be missing
  tomorrow?"

—Hey World, Here I Am!
Jean Little

The Hurt of Death
Is the Price of Love

If you walked into a restaurant and asked for a free dinner, or into a music store and asked for a free CD, or into a grocery store and asked for free cheese, the people in those places would just kick you out, or they might say, "What are you, nuts? Everything here has a price. Nothing is free," and then they would kick you out.

Love has a price, too. That price is the hurt you feel when the person you love dies. You hurt because someone you love has been taken away from you, not for a little while, but for the rest of your life. That hurts. And the more you loved the person who died, the more it will hurt. That's just how love works. That's just the price of love.

The only way not to pay the price of love is never to love anybody, and who wants to live that way? Never loving anybody just because you never want to hurt when love is taken away is silly. In fact, it does not even work, because you then have to live with a different kind of hurt, the hurt of loneliness. So you might as well hurt because you loved, and not because you were afraid to love. Besides, loving and

being loved are the very best feelings any of
us will ever have. You know that somebody else
cares for you and wants to be with you and
wants what is best for you. You know that
you're not alone.

> **The only way not to pay the price
> of love is never to love anybody,
> and who wants to live that way?**

Even though we're sad when the person
we love dies, there is one thing that makes the
sadness hurt a little less. That thing is memory.
We remember love for as long as we live. In
fact, memories of love can even grow stronger
as time goes by. Memory is a great thing.
So because we can remember love always, it
is only the person who died who goes away. The
love that person gave us and that we gave
to him or her will never die, not as long as we
have memory. It is kind of cool. People don't
live forever, but love does live forever; at least
love lives as long as memory lasts. So love
lasts longer than life. That is God's way of
helping us get over the hurt and to get ready to
love the other people in our life just a little bit
more.

During the Civil War, a soldier wrote this letter to his wife not long before he died in the first battle of Bull Run:

My very dear Sarah:
The indications are very strong that we shall move in a few days—perhaps tomorrow. Lest I should not be able to write again, I feel impelled to write a few lines that may fall under your eye when I shall be no more. . . .

Sarah my love for you is deathless, it seems to bind me with mighty cables that nothing but Omnipotence could break; and yet my love of Country comes over me like a strong wind and bears me unresistibly on with all these chains to the battle field.

The memories of the blissful moments I have spent with you come creeping over me, and I feel most gratified to God and to you that I have enjoyed them so long. . . . I have, I know, but few and small claims upon Divine Providence, but something whispers to me . . . that I shall return to my loved ones unharmed. If I do not, my dear Sarah, never forget how much I love you, and when my last breath escapes me on the battle field, it will whisper your name. . . .

But, O Sarah! if the dead can come back to this earth and flit unseen around those they loved, I shall always be near you; in the gladdest days and in the darkest nights . . . always, always, and if there be a soft breeze upon your cheek, it shall be my breath, as the cool air fans your throbbing temple, it shall be my spirit passing by. Sarah do not mourn me dead; think I am gone and wait for thee, for we shall meet again. . . .

—Maj. Sullivan Ballou, 1861

The Three Sadness Steps

Even though we all look different, deep down inside we're pretty much the same. When our bones break, they heal up in pretty much the same way. When our hearts break, the way we get sad and the way we get better is the same for almost everybody. We think of it as being like climbing steps out of a big hole. There are three big steps we all have to climb up to get through the death of somebody we love. We call them "the three sadness steps."

We don't know how long it will take for you to walk up all three sadness steps. It takes some people about a year and it takes some people many years. Even though the steps are the same, the time it takes to climb them is different for each and every grieving person. The main thing is that you have to go up the steps; you can't go around them. Nobody can walk up the steps for you. You have to walk up them yourself. There are no shortcuts to getting over death.

SADNESS STEP #1: SHOCK

The first sadness step is *shock*. You could think of shock as brain fog. Shock fogs your mind so that you can't see anything clearly; you can't really understand what is happening or what to do, or where to go or what to say. Even if you're thinking clearly and you don't feel like you're in a fog, you could still be in shock.

Shock just means that you can't really believe what has just happened. You could also think of shock as like a blanket for your soul. Shock keeps your soul a little warm while everything around you is turning cold. Shock keeps your soul from getting frozen by grief. When you're in shock, you'll say things like "I can't believe this!" or "This isn't real!" A big part of you really does not believe that the person or pet you loved has died. Of course you *know* it; it's just that you can't *feel* it.

SADNESS STEP #2: SEARCHING

Shock does not last forever. Usually after a few weeks or months, you'll begin the second sadness step, which is the step of *searching*. This is the step where you hurt the most. In this step, the shock has gone away and the full hurt and pain of your loss smacks you right in the face. In this second step, you'll feel your loss deep in your soul. The first sadness step is like when you get a deep cut in your finger. You don't feel the worst pain right away, but after a little while—*yikes!*—you *really* feel the pain.

When you're on the second sadness step, you may cry a lot. You may get angry that the person you loved has left you. You may not eat or sleep the way you used to. What is the same for all people in the second sadness step is that the pain is the worst. It's like the time just after you drop the rock on your foot, or like the time just after you fall and break your arm, or like the time just after you know that you're lost.

> **You don't feel the worst pain right away, but after a little while—YIKES!—you REALLY feel the pain.**

In the second sadness step, you'll start searching for some idea or some explanation that will help you understand why this death happened and what you can do about it or learn from it. In the second sadness step, you're searching for an answer, but you're not finding anything! You accept that this death really happened, but you don't understand how it could have happened to someone you love. Death always happens to someone else!

We knew a guy named Clive who got lost in

the jungle hunting for butterflies. Even though Clive was a grown-up, he was still afraid. He kept searching for a way out, and for the longest time he found nothing but more jungle. Then one day a few months later, he walked right out of the jungle and into a big mall that happened to be near the jungle. When people asked Clive if he had ever wanted to give up, Clive answered, "There were lots of days and nights when I searched and found nothing, but I always believed that if I kept searching, some-day I would find my way home." Everybody cheered (and then they took Clive for a jungle burger and a big milk shake). So, if Clive could find his way out of a jungle and into a mall, you can find your way out of the second sadness step. The main thing is never to give up search-ing for a way home.

In the second step, it is very important to have friends and family around you whom you love and trust. When you're in shock, you may not even be aware that people are around you, but when you're in the searching step, you probably will need people to listen to you and comfort you. Don't ever be afraid to ask for help or company when you're in the second step, even if it seems that you're asking for a lot.

When somebody dies, the pain is bad, but when somebody dies and you're alone, the pain is worse. You always know that friends are important, but you have no idea just how important they are until you reach the second sadness step. Your friends may be the ones who help you most to get out of the second sadness step. And the neat thing is that they may help you not by telling you something really wise that you never heard before, but just by being with you and holding your hand and crying with you. When you're in the second sadness step, you may need people more than you need answers.

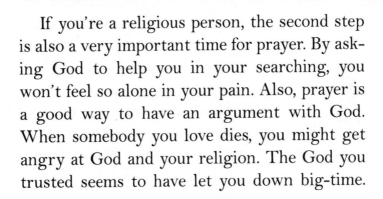

In the second step, it is very important to have friends and family around you whom you love and trust.

If you're a religious person, the second step is also a very important time for prayer. By asking God to help you in your searching, you won't feel so alone in your pain. Also, prayer is a good way to have an argument with God. When somebody you love dies, you might get angry at God and your religion. The God you trusted seems to have let you down big-time.

But we think that God wants us to argue with God because it means that we still believe in God. God can take our anger. God knows that we're in pain and that we don't understand why this death happened. But the God who took the person away from you is also the God who gave that person to you in the first place. Being angry is okay, but also try to remember to be thankful for the time you did have together with that person. If you didn't have much time with the person who died, then maybe God needed that person in heaven more than you needed that person on Earth.

Another good thing to find in the second sadness step is memory. In the middle of being sad for what you'll never have again, it is good to remember what you'll always have and what even death can't take away from you—the memories of the great times you had with the person who died and all the love you once shared together.

> **It is good to remember what you'll always have and what even death can't take away from you.**

SADNESS STEP #3: FINDING

The third sadness step is the step of *finding*. In this step, you'll finally find something to help you get on with your life. In this step, you'll begin to feel kind of, sort of normal again. You'll never feel exactly the same as before the person you loved died, but you'll smile again and laugh again and care about life again. There will still be times when you cry, but you won't cry as much. You'll still get sad, but you won't be sad all the time. During the third sadness step, you may be able to talk about the death and about how you feel. Finally, you'll find a place in your heart to store the pain from the death so that it does not keep you from ever feeling joy again.

In this step, you'll begin to feel kind of, sort of normal again.

Different people find different things in this third step.

Some people find peace by believing that the soul of the person they loved is safe with God in heaven.

Some people find comfort by working with people who are trying to get rid of what caused the death of the person they loved.

Some find that writing about the person helps them to save their memories of love.

Some people find that taking up the hobbies of the person who died helps them feel connected to the person.

Some find that talking to a counselor or a member of the clergy helps them sort out their feelings and get on with their life.

Some find that just letting time pass is what they need in order to feel better.

Some people find that after the death of someone they loved, they don't sweat the small stuff anymore. They realize that how much money you make or what kind of car you drive really doesn't matter. What matters is doing something good with your blessings. What matters is helping people who need help. What matters is never giving up. What matters is giving and getting love.

Finally, you'll find a place to store the pain so that it does not keep you from ever feeling joy again.

Here are some people we have known who found just that very thing:

When Tom's brother Jerry died of AIDS, Tom and his family were very sad. After crying a lot, they decided to raise money to build a house to take care of other people who have AIDS. They named the house Christa House: The Jerry Hartman Residence. MADD (Mothers Against Drunk Driving) is a group started by mothers whose children were killed by drunk drivers. Their work has helped save the lives of many other kids. And when Father Coleman Costello saw a kid die from drugs in the playground across from his church, he spent the rest of his life building houses where kids live and learn how to kick the drug habit. Those houses would not be here except for a death, and a priest who found something important to do because of that death.

These people are heroes and they took giant steps through their sadness steps. They gave courage to others and they used their sadness to make themselves and the world a little better. You can do this, too! But you don't need to be a big hero. You don't need to take giant steps out of your grief. You can take little steps; you can find little things; you can feel better in small ways day by day. And with each little step you take, you'll feel like you're controlling your sadness and not that your sadness is controlling you.

Remember that the finding that happens after death is not finding your way back to how you felt before the person you loved died. You can't go back in life, but you *can* go forward. There is no way around the big things in your life; there is only a way *through* the big things. The sadness steps are the way through sadness to joy, through grief to hope, and through tears to that day when you'll smile again.

FOOTPRINTS

One night a man had a dream. He dreamed he was walking along the beach with the Lord. Across the sky flashed scenes from his life. For each scene, he noticed two sets of footprints in the sand: one belonging to him, and the other to the Lord.

When the last scene of his life flashed before him, he looked back at the footprints in the sand. He noticed that many times along the path of his life there was only one set of footprints. He also noticed that it happened at the very lowest and saddest times in his life.

This really bothered him and he questioned the Lord about it.

"Lord, you said that once I decided to follow you, you'd walk with me all the way. But I have noticed that during the most troublesome times in my life, there is only one set of footprints. I don't understand why when I needed you the most you would leave me."

The Lord replied, "My son, My precious child, I love you and would never leave you. During your times of trial and suffering, when you see only one set of footprints, it was then that I carried you."

—*Anonymous*

Time Heals All Wounds

When you break your arm and the doctor puts it in a cast, you can't make it heal by yelling or screaming or crying or jumping around like a wild animal. You just have to wait for the bones to take their own sweet time to get better. You just need to be patient with your bones and give them time to heal. Well, it is the same with a broken heart, which is what you have after somebody you love dies. You need to be patient with your grief. There is an old saying: Time heals all wounds. We believe it's true and that it's worth remembering when somebody you

love has died. Time is a great healer for broken bones and broken hearts.

But sometimes the person grieving gets impatient to be healed way before it is time to be healed. Impatient people seem to have the hardest time getting rid of grief. They want to get back to normal and get on with their lives. They want to be happy again, and they want it now! Well, wanting it does not make it happen. Patience in the face of grief is the only way to let time heal our wounds.

But if you lead a lonely life, all the time in the world won't heal you. Stuffed into your time, you need love, friends, and birthdays and holidays with your family. You need to walk on the beach with puppy dogs and hear the crunch of leaves on a crisp fall day. You need to taste hot fudge sundaes and hard, juicy apples picked right from the tree. If your time is filled with these kinds of things, then you'll slowly remember how good life is, even with all the death that is sprinkled through it. You'll remember how death is really a part of life. You may then find your way back to believing that God loves and protects us all, even if we don't believe it or know it. All those things *plus* time will heal all our wounds.

The other important thing to remember about

time healing all wounds is that we don't get healed in a straight line. We don't get a little better every single day until we're well again. The way time heals our wounds is an up-and-down thing. You can go for days or weeks or even months getting better and better after somebody you love has died, and then suddenly—*wham!*—something happens that makes you almost as sad as you were on the day the person died. This is really weird but very normal. Healing is like sailing in a storm. You'll bounce around a lot, going up and down the waves, until at last the storm passes and you come home again. But don't worry. The storm will pass. You'll heal. You'll heal.

Now his mother came to say good night.

"Why does the day have to end?" he asked her.

"So night can begin," she said, "look."

She pointed out the window where, high in the darkening sky, behind the branches of the pear tree, the little boy could see a pale sliver of moon.

"That's the night beginning," his mother said, resting her hand on his shoulder, "the night with the moon and

stars and darkness for you to dream in."

"But where does the sun go when the day ends?" the little boy asked.

"The day doesn't end," said his mother, "it begins somewhere else. The sun will be shining there, when night begins here. Nothing ends."

"Nothing?" the little boy asked.

"Nothing," his mother said. "It begins in another place or in a different way."

—When the Wind Stops
Charlotte Zolotow

The Ways
Death Comes

There are four main ways that death happens to someone: Death can come suddenly, or death can come slowly. Death can be painful, or death can be peaceful. All the ways bring death, but each is very different and each has something big to teach us about life and death.

Sudden Death

When the death of somebody you love comes fast and without warning, like when a person dies in an accident, the first sadness step of shock is bigger and longer than when the person you loved was sick for a long time and died from an illness. It is never easy to get ready for death, but when you know death is coming, it is a little easier to accept. But when you say good-bye to a healthy, wonderful person in the morning and then they die in some terrible accident by the afternoon, it's like being hit from behind by a big hard punch. You don't see it coming, but you sure feel the pain. Your life goes from normal to broken in about one second.

It is never easy to get ready for death, but when you know death is coming, it is a little easier to accept.

Sudden death is also hard because you don't have a chance to say, "Good-bye, I love you." The last words you might have said to the person could have been, "Don't forget to pick me up after practice tonight," or "We need more Rice Krispies." You have no time to tie up loose ends, to share memories, to make up for old silly fights. In sudden deaths, everything is a mess, nobody is ready, and probably everyone is freaking out. If it was an accident that caused the sudden death, then you may be angry at the person who may have caused the accident, or maybe you even feel crazy anger at the people who tried but couldn't save the person after the accident. All most people can think about after sudden death is how it shouldn't have happened and whose fault it is that it did.

But sudden death, as hard and terrible as it is, has things about it that are easier than some of the other ways death comes. Your loved one was not sick and didn't have to spend years suffering. There are no long stays in the hospital, no painful operations, no expensive medicines, no tubes and machines. Many people are afraid of dying slowly because they don't want to burden the people they love. People who die suddenly just go from being alive to being dead, and when you think about how much pain many people have when they die, dying suddenly is a blessing in that way.

There are things you can learn from the sudden death of a loved one that can help you for the rest of your life. You can find that each day is a gift. When you think of every day as a gift, a little prize you find every morning in your cereal, then you'll not let any day go by without saying, "Thank you, God, for this day." You'll not want to sit around like a couch potato figuring that you have lots of other days to get something good done for yourself, for your family, for your country, and for your world. But most importantly, you'll not want to let any day go by without saying "I love you" to the people you love.

> *What is life? It is the flash of a firefly in the night. It is the breath of a buffalo in the wintertime. It is the little shadow which runs across the grass and loses itself in the sunset.*
>
> —*Crowfoot, Canadian Blackfoot Indian chief, 1890*

Slow Death

Slow death seems like it would be a lot easier than sudden death, but it is also hard. When the person you love is sick with some disease and it takes a long time for them to die, everyone has time to tie up all the loose ends of that person's life. That is a good thing. There is time to tell the person just how much you love him or her. There is time to patch up old silly arguments and grudges and jealousies. There is time for the person to give away things so that people won't fight over them later. There may also be time to do some good that the sick person had put off while he or she was busy and well. Many sick people have written beautiful books or painted wonderful paintings or put down the story of their lives so that their great-grand-children can know where they came from.

But slow death is also hard because there is often a lot of pain that comes with it. The person sometimes loses his or her abilities slowly, until there is not much of the person left. Maybe the person is dying slowly of an illness that takes away memory, like Alzheimer's disease. A slowly dying person also need lots of help from friends and family. Sometimes it is hard for these helpers to find the time to help the dying person and still do all the other things the people in their lives need them to do. Many people just don't like to visit dying people because they don't know what to say. The funny thing is that most dying people we have known don't care if their visitors say anything. They're just happy to have people they love spend time with them.

The biggest good thing you can find when somebody you know is dying slowly is that it gives you a chance to repay the love you got from that person. When people love you, they don't ever expect you to pay them back for that love. Their love for you is free. But with a slow death, you get the chance to give back some of the love and caring that the sick person gave to you.

Being with a slowly dying person is a sad but joyful burden. It is a tiring but holy job. It is the way you show that you care for more than just yourself.

Shortly before his death from cancer in 1996, a very caring man named Joseph Cardinal Bernardin wrote the following:

It is the first day of November, and fall is giving way to winter. Soon the trees will lose the vibrant colors of their leaves and snow will cover the ground. The earth will shut down, and people will race to and from their destinations bundled up for warmth. . . . Winters are harsh. It is a time of dying. But we know that spring will soon come with all its new life and wonder. It is quite clear that I will not be alive then. But I will soon experience new life in a different way. Although I do not know what to expect in the afterlife, I do know that just as God has called me to serve him to the best of my ability

*throughout my life on earth, he is now
calling me home.*

—The Gift of Peace
Joseph Cardinal Bernardin

Painful Death

Painful deaths can be short or they can be long, but they're by far the worst kinds of death. Doctors know a lot more today about how to get rid of pain than they did in the old days, but some diseases bring so much pain that medicine cannot do very much. But even so, you *can* find something even in the middle of great pain that will be a great lesson for your life.

Many people find that peaceful thoughts or meditation can relax them; they use the power of their minds to stop the pain they feel. Prayer is another way to deal with pain. It is really amazing how many people believe that praying to get rid of pain is very powerful. We pray for sick people all the time, and sometimes we have seen miracles happen that even science can't explain.

Touching is another way people deal with pain. Holding hands with somebody who is sick helps take away pain from that person. Brushing their hair or rubbing their back or feet or face can help them find something good in the middle of pain. We knew a woman who was dying of cancer, and one day a bunch of her friends went over to her house and gave her a manicure. They filed her nails and painted them her favorite color. At the end of the manicure, she looked up at them and smiled her biggest smile. During that time, she had no pain, and a little red nail polish and some smiles were all it took.

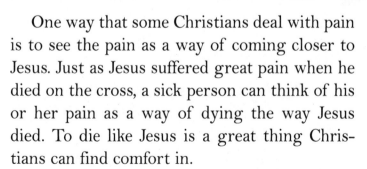

Holding hands with somebody who is sick helps take away pain from that person.

One way that some Christians deal with pain is to see the pain as a way of coming closer to Jesus. Just as Jesus suffered great pain when he died on the cross, a sick person can think of his or her pain as a way of dying the way Jesus died. To die like Jesus is a great thing Christians can find comfort in.

One other thing about pain: It is okay to pray for the death of somebody who is in pain. It is not a bad prayer. It is a good and kind prayer, and when there is no hope that the person can get well, you can pray that God will come and end the suffering today and not tomorrow.

We don't understand why God lets people suffer so much pain before they die. When God takes us away and brings our souls to heaven, and after we get our wings and halos and get our places to hang out, the very first question we're going to ask God is, "Why did you allow so much pain in the world?" When we find out the answer, we'll try to call you from heaven and let you know. Until then, pain is just the biggest mystery and the hardest lost-and-found lesson ever.

> The Twenty-third Psalm has a comforting way of helping us through painful death and all death. It is so full of hope that the hope just floods our pain with love.
>
> *The Lord is my shepherd, I shall not*
>   *want; he makes me lie down in green*
>   *pastures.*
> *He leads me beside still waters; he*
>   *restores my soul.*
> *He leads me in paths of righteousness*
>   *for his name's sake.*

*Even though I walk through the valley
of the shadow of death, I fear no
evil; for thou art with me; thy rod
and thy staff, they comfort me.
Thou preparest a table before me in the
presence of my enemies; thou
anointest my head with oil, my cup
overflows.
Surely goodness and mercy shall follow
me all the days of my life; and I
shall dwell in the house of the Lord
for ever.*

Peaceful Death

Peaceful death is what we all pray for. Nobody wants to die with pain. Nobody wants to die angry. Nobody wants to die afraid. Dying peacefully is the best way to go, and when it happens to somebody you love, make sure you thank God right away for such a blessing.

Dying peacefully gives a person the chance to gather his or her family around and tell each of them how much they were loved and what the dying person hoped for each of them. Dying peacefully gives a person the chance to plan the

funeral and to ask certain people to speak at it.
It allows the person to say what he or she wants
people to do to remember him or her, or just to
hold hands one last time and to give one last
kiss to loved ones.

We should tell you how we think people
really die, whether it's sudden or slow, painful
or peaceful. We think that when you die, you
first feel your soul coming loose from your
body. You see that there is something wonderful waiting for you and you're absolutely not
afraid of anything. You see the light of God and

you hear the souls of those people you have loved calling to you and welcoming you into the world to come. But you're not dead yet. You're not dead until God comes right up to you, very close, and kisses you on the lips and takes your breath away. Then you go to a place where everything is found and nothing is ever lost.

IN HARDWOOD GROVES

The same leaves over and over again!
They fall from giving shade above
To make one texture of faded brown
And fit the earth like a leather glove.

Before the leaves can mount again
To fill the trees with another shade,
They must go down past things coming up.
They must go down into the dark
*   decayed.*

They must be pierced by flowers and put
Beneath the feet of dancing flowers.
However it is in some other world
I know that this is the way in ours.

—Robert Frost

The Ones
We Lose

No matter who dies and no matter when they die, if you loved that person or that animal, it's going to hurt. But the hurt is different for each person or living thing you loved—and with every different type of death, there are different ways you may need to heal. Hurting when somebody you love dies is a good thing because it means you loved and were loved in your life. Knowing this does not take away the pain, but it does help you to accept it and makes it easier for you to be happy again someday.

Losing a Pet

Pets are like members of your family. In fact, your pet might be nicer than some people in your family. Pets are fuzzy and cuddly or slimy and interesting. Pets follow you around or wait until you lie down and then jump all over you. Pets sing to you or howl at you. They lick you or rub up against you or guard your house from burglars (or they just lick the burglars the same way they lick you and let them take everything in your house).

You may have picked out your pet and you may have named it, but the most special thing about pets is that they need you to live. It is a big responsibility to have some other living thing depend upon you for life. Later on in your life, you might have your own children, who will also need you to take care of them. You may not think that feeding your goldfish is good practice for feeding your kids someday, but it is. (Of course, you'll need to remember not to drop your kid's peanut butter and jelly sandwiches into the fish tank or they'll clog up the filters.)

So for all these reasons, it is a sad thing when a pet dies. For some people, the death of a pet is just like the death of someone in the family. For many people who live alone, a pet is their only companion and the death of their pet means that they're *really* alone.

The big thing about losing a pet is that you get to see a whole life from beginning to end. It

kind of gives you a fast-forward look at your
own life and the lives of the people you love.
You get to see your pet when it is a baby animal,
then a teenager, later a grown-up, then old and
sick, and finally dead. It is just the way it happens to humans, except humans live a lot longer.
People say one dog year is like seven of our
years, and so that means most dogs, in ten or fif-
teen years, live the equal of a normal human life
span. By seeing how your pet lives and grows
and dies, you learn about how all life, including
ours, does the same thing. Pets get us ready to
deal with death because they usually die first.

Lots of kids ask us if their pets go to heaven

when they die. We believe that God will take care of all the animals. We also believe that God has a special place in heaven for the animals who give us love and even for the animals who give us food. We believe that all life will be safe with God.

> **By seeing how your pet lives and grows and dies, you learn about how all life, including ours, does the same thing.**

If your pet dies, you may want to have some kind of a funeral. You may want to bury your pet yourself, or you may want to have a few of the people who knew your pet come over to your house and say some prayers or look at pictures or tell stories about your pet that will make everyone smile. Maybe you could put some of those pictures of your pet and some of your pet's favorite toys or your pet's collar into a memory box that you could put on your shelf. Then, when you want to remember your pet, you can just open the memory box and go through the pictures and touch the toys and you'll feel close to your pet again.

Another good thing to do is to get a new pet that will take away some of the sadness you feel. It will give you another living thing to take care of and to love. New love is the only cure we know for losing old love, and once you learn that there is always some new living thing that wants to be loved and wants to love you, you'll have found a very big thing after losing a very big thing, and that is what lost and found is all about.

Barney was brave, I said.
And smart and funny and clean.
Also cuddly and handsome, and he only
*   once ate a bird.*
It was sweet, I said, to hear him purr in
*   my ear.*
And sometimes he slept on my belly and
*   kept it warm.*

Those are all good things, said my
*   mother, but I still just count nine.*

Yes, I said, but now I have another.

Barney is in the ground and he's helping
*   grow flowers.*
You know, I said, that's a pretty nice job
*   for a cat.*

—The Tenth Good Thing about Barney
Judith Viorst

Losing a Grandpa or Grandma

Grandparents had practice raising your parents before they got to you, so this makes helping to raise you a piece of cake. Grandparents are terrific people to have in your life. Maybe they let you eat food you can't eat at home. Maybe they took you to the amusement park, where they let you go on the ride that turned you around and around until you threw up. Maybe they told you stories about your mom and dad that your parents were too embarrassed to tell you. Maybe your grandparents taught you about your religion or about your ancestors or about the country your family came from before they came to America. Maybe your grandparents even taught you the right thing to do or scolded you when you did the wrong thing. Most of all, your grandparents probably gave you a special love that no other people on the whole earth could give to you.

Your grandparents are probably so much older than you that there is a good chance that you'll be alive when your grandpa or grandma dies; in fact, there is also a chance that you'll still be a kid when they die. And when one of your grandparents dies, it will be a huge loss for you, for your mom and dad, and for your whole family. You'll all go through each of the three sadness steps, but with the death of a grandparent, some things about the sadness steps are easier and some things are harder.

The easier thing about the death of a grandparent is that you can remind yourself that your grandparent lived a pretty long life. Nobody lives forever, but your grandparents have lived closer to forever than you have. You can give thanks to God for all the years of life your grandma or grandpa had. You can be thankful that your grandparents saw their children grow up, and you can give extra-special thanks that they saw the child of their children (who is *you*) begin to grow, too. These are big things to be thankful for and they help take away some of the pain.

The harder thing about the death of a grandparent is that this death means that you have to see close-up the way your family grows and changes. It changed for good when you were born, and it changes for bad when your grandparents die. But we *all* grow up. We all get older, and we go from being the baby of the family to being one of the kids, then to being one of the teenagers, to being one of the uncles or aunts, to being one of the married people, to being one of the parents, to being one of the grandparents, and then when we're one of the oldest people in the family, it is our time to die and go to heaven.

It's kind of like flowers. Flowers are pretty and colorful, but they're also seed holders. After the flower makes its seeds grow, it has done its job and it is ready to fall off the stem and die, but the seeds live on and they make new flowers next spring. Now, people are not flowers. Flowers get old and ugly and people can stay pretty to the end of a big long life. Flowers are only here to make new flowers, but people can make songs and paintings and the perfect apple pie. But in one way, we're like flowers. We all have our season to bloom. We all have our time in the sun, and we should try to be just as beautiful and colorful and fragrant as we can before the winter comes. It would be nice if flowers bloomed forever, but then there would never be a need for any new flowers. It's just not nature's way to let flowers live forever, and it's the same with people.

Your grandpa and grandma are colorful flowers that have been in the garden for a long time, but the time comes when they'll go back to the earth. But only the bodies of your grandparents return to the earth. The really great parts of them, their souls, go right up to God to watch over you and to wait for you until your season in the sun is over.

That's the big thing you can find in the death of a grandparent—the way death is a normal part of life. When somebody your own age dies, like a friend or a brother or a sister, it's not normal. (It isn't even normal for your parents to die, because even though they're older than you are, they're still not that old.) But it *is* normal for grandparents to die. They came into this world before you, so it is normal and natural for them to leave this world before you. It is the best way to discover that it is normal and natural for people to grow old and die.

When your grandparents die, you can also find out something about your history that maybe you never knew. After all, you didn't come from just any people; you came from *these* people. If you take time with them while they're alive, you can learn what it means to be a part of your family and what stories you should know. Your grandparents are your living history, and one thing you can do before they die is to get that history told to you. At their funeral, people can tell you family stories, but it is better to hear the stories from them when they can end each one with a hug and a kiss.

Another thing you can find out after your grandparents die is how to comfort your parents. You're sad because your grandpa or grandma has just died, but think about how your parents are feeling. They just lost their mom or dad (or their father-in-law or mother-in-law). You might even see your parents cry for the very first time, or they might not have as much time for you when they're busy making

all the funeral arrangements. Maybe they'll
even seem angry at times, but they're not angry
at you.

In those times, your parents need a hug.
They need somebody to say, "I love you and
don't worry. Everything will be all right"—just
like you need to hear that when you're sad.
When you do this, you'll not only comfort
them; you'll grow up in a great big way.
Learning how to help the ones you love when
they're sad is a huge thing to learn—and when
you learn it, you may be a kid in years, but
you're a big grown-up person where it counts
the most.

> *"I thought people didn't do anything but
> cry for weeks when somebody died," I
> said after a long while. "But I had fun
> sometimes at Grandma's funeral."*
>
> *"I had a good time, too," said Mom.
> "That's one of the things that funerals are
> for. We said good-bye to Grandma, and
> we said hello to our family and friends."*
>
> *"Grandma would have enjoyed it
> more than anyone," said Dad. "She loved
> to gather everybody 'round and cook a
> feast."*

> *We talked about the dinners Grandma used to cook. I thought about her sitting on the dock to watch the sun go down, and cooking the bass she'd caught so they'd melt on your tongue before you had a chance to chew.*
>
> *Then I fell asleep and dreamed about taking the train to visit Grandpa in a month. We would talk about Grandma and remember the ways things used to be. He would teach me fishing, and we would learn together how to cook.*
>
> —Saying Good-bye to Grandma
> *Jane Resh Thomas*

Losing a Mom or Dad

You didn't come from nowhere. You came from somewhere, and that somewhere is from your mom and dad. When your mom or dad dies, a big part of your somewhere is taken away. Even if you were adopted, your mom and dad are still the place your biggest love comes from. They're the ones who teach you the right way to live. They're the most important teachers you'll ever have in your life.

Moms and dads patch up your boo-boos when you're little and your boo-boos are just scratches on your knee, or when you're older and your boo-boo is not getting asked to the school dance, or when you're much older and your boo-boo might be losing your job. They're there to see you play soccer or sing in the school play. They're there to hold your own child and give that child all the love they once gave to you. The longer you live, the more you'll understand about how you became what you are mainly because of them.

It is always hard to lose a mom or dad, but if you're a kid, it is extra hard. You need a mom or dad in a deeper way when you're a kid because you need your parent to help you get grown-up. If your mom or dad dies, the big question you're going to wonder about is Who is going to take care of me? Well, don't worry. *Somebody* will definitely take care of you. If you still have one parent alive, that parent will take care of you. If both your parents die, maybe an aunt or an uncle or a friend of the family will take care of you. Just remember you're not alone and you have nothing to fear, even if your life is really different for a while.

When your parents die, the three sadness steps can be especially big and long. During the second step, it is very normal for you to be angry and not just sad. You're angry because you feel that it is not fair for you to lose somebody you love so much who was so good to you. You're angry because you may feel like your biggest helper has been taken away from you at just the time in your life when you need help the most.

Lots of kids whose parents die also feel

guilty about the death. They may remember yelling at their parents or lying to them, and they think that maybe if they hadn't done those things, their parents would still be alive. Well, we don't know everything, but one thing we know for sure is that you didn't do anything to cause the death of your parent. In fact, you're probably the main reason why your parent wanted to live.

The third sadness step may take a long time, too. You may be just sad and blue for most of a year before you even *want* to find something to help you deal with the death of your mom or dad. That's okay. Remember to have patience with your grief. Someday it will go away enough for you to go on with your life and find joy once again. It is a great thing to find out how that strength and love and patience inside of you will get you through the really hard times in your life. When you get through this, you'll be much stronger and much more loving because you'll trust in your ability to heal up even after your heart breaks.

When your parent dies, you have the chance to grow up and do some of the wonderful things your mom or dad did for your family.

Maybe your mom or your dad was the one who called people on their birthday. Now you can be the birthday caller. Maybe your mom or dad was the one who always made peace in the family. Well, maybe you can grow up to be the peacemaker someday. Nobody can replace anybody, but everybody can help to do some of the good things the person who died used to do.

> **You may be sad for a year before you even WANT to find something to help you deal with the death.**

Maybe the death of your parents will help you find a way to grow closer to your brothers and sisters. Maybe you'll learn that fighting about who gets the remote control or who gets to sit in the front seat is silly. You really need one another to get through this death. Coming closer to the people in your family would be a big find.

Families are like a board with nails pounded in it and rubber bands stretched over the nails. Those rubber bands make a pattern. If you pull out one of the nails, the pattern of the rubber bands is suddenly different. It's the same when your mom or dad dies. Your parent was one of the nails of your family, and without that person, your family has a new shape. But you're one of the nails left in the board, and doing your best to help everybody learn to live with the new shape of the family is a very great thing to do.

You might also find stories. Stories about your mom and dad are what keep their memories alive. You know some stories about them because they told you, but we bet that if you ask your uncles or aunts or your parents' friends, you'll find stories about them that you didn't know. You can write them down in a book of remembrances. You can tell them to your children someday. Stories help you fill in the holes that the death opens up in your life. Besides, many of the stories will make you smile. And smiling is one of the most important first steps toward healing that you can find.

> *Hope is like the sun, which, as we journey toward it, casts the shadow of our burden behind us.*
>
> —*Samuel Smiles*

Losing a Brother or Sister

It's not natural to see your brother or sister die when you're a kid. They're close to your age, and they're supposed to grow up with you and have children of their own, who will be your nieces and nephews. You're growing up with them, and you deserve the chance to keep growing with them for the rest of your life. But life does not always give you what you deserve.

If your brother or sister was older than you, he or she probably taught you things your parents never would teach you, like how to swear and belch, or how to dress, or how to play ball, or how to get girls or boys, or how to get through Mrs. Farkas's math class. Maybe your sibling loaned you money or took you to games or let you hang with his or her friends as long as you were not a total dweeb.

If the brother or sister who died was younger than you, there was a different bond between the two of you. You were the one who taught your brother or sister. You were the one who protected him or her. You were the one who baby-sat. You might think that there was something you could have done to save your brother or sister from death because you saved

him or her from getting beaten up by Craig Schwartz.

The death of a brother or sister is hard because he or she is not in your life anymore. That means no more playing with you or helping you with homework or just talking with you about important and silly things. And as if the death of a brother or sister were not bad enough, you might also start thinking the scary thought that if your brother or sister could die, that means *you* or anybody else in your family could die, too.

Another tough thing about the death of a brother or sister is that it can totally wreck your parents for a long while. It may seem like they don't have much time for you after the death of your brother or sister because they're so sad themselves and may need time alone to get through it. It might be hard for them to comfort you because they can't even comfort themselves. You're used to seeing your parents strong, and when a brother or sister dies, you're going to see your parents as weak as they can be.

What can you find when your brother or sister dies?

One thing you can find is a way to treat all your other brothers and sisters, if you have any, with extra love. It is very common for brothers and sisters to fight a lot, but underneath the fighting is a lot of love (it's just that we don't always show the love and we usually show the anger). The death of a brother or sister will remind you of just how much you really do love your siblings. So learn how to share with them and care for them and cut them some slack. It makes fighting about their eating the candy bar you were saving in the freezer just silly (which you knew anyway). The death of a loved one shows you what really matters in life.

Another thing to think about is how lucky you were to have a brother or a sister in the first place. There are lots of kids who don't have any brothers and sisters, and these kids will never know what it is like to steal a sister's sweater or listen in when a brother calls his girlfriend. They don't have anyone to drive them to the movies, so that they would not be embarrassed by having their parents drive (which is nowhere near as cool as having a brother or sister drive you). They have nobody to tell them the truth about how their shirt or haircut looks.

And they have nobody who at the end of a long, hard day can come into their room and sit on their bed and see that they're blitzed and put a hand on their shoulder and say, "I know just how you feel." And even though moms and dads and grandpas and grandmas sit on your bed and say the same thing, you kind of believe it more when a brother or sister says it to you. You had that special gift with your brother or sister, and even if you don't have it now, at least you had it for a while.

> *As a well-spent day brings happy sleep, so life well used brings happy death.*
>
> —*Leonardo da Vinci*

Losing a Friend

Since you're a kid and your friends are also kids, the death of one of your friends is not going to happen often (if it happens at all). Just like your brothers and sisters, most of your friends are going to grow up and get old with you. That's the way it usually happens, and when it does not happen that way, it is a terrible shock.

Friends can talk you out of doing stupid things and they can get you to do stupid things. Friends can walk home from school with you or ride home on the bus with you and still want to call you up when they get home because you have more stuff to talk about. Friends can care for you when you don't even care for yourself. Friends can understand you and help you to understand yourself. Friends are one of the best things about life here on planet Earth, and when one of your friends dies, it is a very great and painful loss.

When a friend dies, you may be really angry that a good young person who should have been able to grow up, get married, have kids, get old, and fall asleep on the couch died too soon—*way* too soon. You may feel frustrated that there is nothing you can do to bring the person back to

life. You may feel guilty that maybe there was
something you did that hurt your friend. You
may feel abandoned. It's just not that easy to go
out there and replace a friend! You may be
afraid that if your friend died, maybe you might
die, too. You may not believe in God for a while
because you just don't understand why God
would take your friend when God has so many
creeps to take instead. Most of all, you'll be sad
and confused because a person you took for
granted as being in your life just disappeared
forever.

When a friend dies, many kids who were also

friends of your friend are
going to be very upset, too.
Even kids who didn't know
your friend that well may
be upset. The death of a
child upsets the whole
community in which you
live. This will make your
going to school sad and it
will make it hard to study
or go on with things in a
normal way. Your school
will probably let you and
your friends see a coun-

selor who can help you talk about how you feel.
Together, you can get strength to help one
another.

It is a good thing to go to your friend's
funeral and maybe to have some service at the
school where kids can speak and remember
your friend. You could also write a letter to
your friend's family and tell them how you feel
and that you hope God will comfort them.

In time, you'll move on with your life and
find new friends, but you'll always have a place
in your heart where the love you had for your
friend can live forever . . . and ever.

DEAR
Lord—

Please
give me
the strength
to try

the strength
to laugh
the strength
to cry

the strength
to hope
the strength
to cope

the strength
to one day
say good-bye
to fly
into
a
brighter
sky.

It's good
to know
You're
always there—

that
I can
share with You
this prayer.

Thank You
for listening
once again.

Good night
Dear Lord,

Amen.

Amen.

—Been to Yesterdays: Poems of a Life
Lee Bennett Hopkins

PART III

The Good in Good-bye

*We are lonely . . .
until we find ourselves.*

—*Proverb*

The Good in Good-bye

Everybody has lost *some* of the things we write about in this book. If you have lost all of the things in this book already, the first thing you have to admit is that you have *really* bad luck. But there is one important lesson that can come to you only if you have lost something or somebody you love: *Losing is the only way to get wise!*

Being smart is not the same as being wise. Smart comes from having a big brain. Wise comes from having a big heart. You can't decide if you'll be smart. God decides that, and your parents had a little something to do with it, too. Being smart means *knowing what is.* Being wise means *knowing what really matters.* And you become wise only after you lose someone or something that really matters.

Now, some people lose lots of things and

they never get wise. They only get angry and bitter and they go around moping about how life isn't fair. The people who get wise from their losses are the ones who see everything that happens to them as a chance—a chance to grow, a chance to learn, a chance to become wise. What you lose is not in your control, but what you find is!

> **Being smart means KNOWING WHAT IS.**
> **Being wise means KNOWING**
> **WHAT REALLY MATTERS.**

The losing that you thought was so bad turns out to be the very thing that helps you grow up. You can be a grown-up when you're just nine, and you can be a kid when you're ninety-five. Being grown has more to do with how wise you are than how old you are. It really is your choice whether you find something and get a little bit wiser after you lose something or whether you stay clueless all your life. When you add up everything you lose and everything you find, the amazing thing is that what you find weighs more than what you lose. It may hurt to lose what we love or need, but our hurts make us who we are. Our hurts help us to grow up, and growing up is a good thing.

Most kids tell us that they're glad to grow up. When you're a kid, there are lots of good things—you don't have to get a job or pay rent or wash your own clothes—but there are tough things that come with being a kid, too. You can't set your own bedtime. You can't have parties in the house without asking permission. You can't drive a car (except with your mom or dad in your own driveway, and there are not that many interesting places to visit in your driveway). You can't have chocolate and cookies and gum for dinner, and, worst of all, some grown-up is *always* telling you what to do.

People who can lift or pull lots of weight are strong people, but the strongest people are those with *inner strength*. Inner strength is the strength you get through a loss. Just like lifting weights and exercising is the only way to get big muscles, losing things you love is the only way to get inner strength. Losing is like gym class for your guts. Nobody gets big muscles after one day at the gym and nobody gets strong on the inside after just one loss. It takes a lot of living and a lot of losing and a lot of finding to get to the place where you're as strong and loving, as good and kind, as happy and patient as you could ever be. But we know that you'll get to that place of peace. We believe in you!

We hope that our words have given you some good ideas of how to deal with losing what you love. We know that we didn't answer all your questions, but we have some big news for you: *There is no way to answer most of the questions in this book.* The big questions about life and death, about losing and finding, are not like math problems. They stay with you as long as you live. So we need to try to *live* with the questions, not try so hard to *answer* the questions. If we learn to live with the questions, then someday, without even realizing when it happens or how it happens, we'll live our way into the answers.

> *Amazing grace! How sweet the sound*
> *That saved a wretch like me!*
> *I once was lost, but now am found,*
> *Was blind, but now I see.*

Through many dangers, toils, and snares
I have already come;
'Tis grace that brought me safe thus far,
And grace will lead me home.

—*"Amazing Grace"*
Capt. John Newton

Further Reading

Nonfiction Books

Bratman, Fred. *Everything You Need to Know When a Parent Dies.* New York: Rosen Publishing Group, 1992. Offers advice on how children may deal with the pain and loss of a parent and what friends can do to help with the process of grieving.

Fry, Virginia Lynn. *Part of Me Died, Too: Stories of Creative Survival among Children and Teenagers.* New York: Dutton, 1995. Fry relates the stories of eleven kids, from preschool to eighteen, who are coping with the death of a pet, a grandparent, a parent, a sibling, or a friend.

Gravelle, Karen, and Charles Haskins. *Teenagers Face to Face with Bereavement.* Englewood Cliffs, New Jersey: Julian Messner, 1989. Seventeen adolescents who have lost a parent, brother, sister, or close friend talk about the stages of grief and how to handle the funeral; going back to school; and depression, pain, anger, and guilt.

Heegaard, Marge Eaton. *Coping with Death and Grief.* Minneapolis: Lerner Publications, 1990. Heegaard helps children deal with saying good-bye to persons who are dying, letting out feelings, helping another person to grieve, and feeling good about oneself.

Krementz, Jill. *How It Feels When a Parent Dies.* New York: Alfred A. Knopf, 1992. Eighteen kids, ages seven to sixteen, describe their feelings of loss after the deaths of their mothers or fathers as a result of illnesses, accidents, or suicides.

Roehm, Michelle, compiler. *Girls Know Best: Advice for Girls from Girls on Just about Everything!* Hillsboro, Oregon: Beyond Words, 1997. Thirty-eight girl authors, ages seven to sixteen, offer advice on siblings, surviving divorce, depression, friendships, and overcoming life's biggest challenges, among other topics.

Rofres, Eric E., editor. *The Kids' Book about Death and Dying.* New York: Little, Brown, 1985. Fourteen kids, ages eleven to fourteen, offer their insights about what death is, funeral customs, when pets die, different types of death, and whether there is life after death.

Fiction Books

Bauer, Joan. *Rules of the Road.* New York: Putnam, 1998. An unusual summer job and the untimely death of a new friend bring sixteen-year-old Genna strength, independence, and insight into herself and her usually absent and alcoholic father.

Buscaglia, Leo. *The Fall of Freddie the Leaf: A Story of Life for All Ages.* New York: Henry Holt, 1982. Dedicated to children who have suffered loss, this book uses the renewing cycle of the four seasons to illustrate life and death.

Calvert, Patricia. *Picking Up the Pieces.* New York: Scribner's, 1993. Megan begins to rebuild her life after a motorcycle accident that leaves her paralyzed.

Cleary, Beverly. *Dear Mr. Henshaw.* New York: Morrow Junior Books, 1983. Ten-year-old Leigh reveals his problems with his parents' divorce and being the new kid in school in letters to his favorite author, Boyd Henshaw.

Dessen, Sarah. *That Summer.* New York: Orchard Books, 1996. During the summer of her sister's wedding, a young girl comes to grips with the divorce of her parents, her father's remarriage, and her sister's leaving home.

Gardiner, John Reynolds. *Stone Fox.* New York: HarperCollins, 1980. Little Willie learns the meaning of sacrifice when his beloved dog, Searchlight, dies during a dogsled race to save the family farm.

Gordon, Ruth, compiler. *Pierced by a Ray of Sun: Poems about the Times We Feel Alone.* New York: HarperCollins, 1995. An anthology of poetry selected with the hope that readers may draw comfort in the sameness of our loneliness.

Lowry, Lois. *A Summer to Die.* Boston: Houghton Mifflin, 1977. Thirteen-year-old Meg must deal not only with her feelings of jealousy toward her older sister Molly but also with guilt and grief as Molly becomes ill and dies.

Park, Barbara. *Mick Harte Was Here.* New York: Alfred A. Knopf, 1995. As thirteen-year-old Phoebe recalls her younger brother Mick and his death in a bicycle accident, she finds she is able to take the first step in recovering from her terrible loss.

Roberts, Willo Davis. *Secrets at Hidden Valley.* New York: Atheneum, 1997. The sudden death of eleven-year-old Steffi's father is made more difficult when she feels her mother abandons her for the summer to a disagreeable grandfather she has never met.

Voigt, Cynthia. *Izzy, Willy-Nilly*. New York: Atheneum, 1986. After the loss of her leg in a car wreck, Izzy finds she must learn to handle the emotional changes in her life as well as the physical ones.

A Few Other Resources

Concerned Counseling (888-415-TALK or www.concernedcounseling.com) is a twenty-four-hour service with licensed professional counselors who provide confidential help with grief, loss, loneliness, and other problems. Parental permission is required for children to use this service.

The Delta Society (800-869-6898 or www.deltasociety.org) provides counselors, telephone hot lines, and support groups throughout the United States to deal with pet loss. A complimentary bibliography is available.

Cancer Kids (www.cancerkids.org) helps children with cancer tell their stories to the world.

Acknowledgments

Leigh Ann Jones and Marian Reiner are gratefully acknowledged for their contributions to this project.

Excerpt from *The Gift of Peace*, by Joseph Cardinal Bernardin. Copyright © 1996 by Loyola Press, Chicago. Reprinted by permission of Loyola Press.

Excerpt from *Picking Up the Pieces*, by Patricia Calvert. Copyright © 1993 by Patricia Calvert. Reprinted with the permission of Atheneum Books for Young Readers, an imprint of Simon & Schuster Children's Publishing Divison.

Excerpt from *That Summer*, by Sarah Dessen. Copyright © 1996 by Sarah Dessen. Reprinted by permission of Orchard Books, New York.

Excerpt from *Anne Frank: The Diary of a Young Girl*, by Anne Frank. Copyright © 1952 by Otto H. Frank. Used by permission of Doubleday, a division of Bantam Doubleday Dell Publishing Group, Inc.

"In Hardwood Groves" from *The Poetry of Robert Frost*, edited by